Let's Enjoy Maste...

Heidi

海蒂
阿爾卑斯山的小女孩

Original Author   Johanna Spyri
Adaptor   Andrew Chien
Proofreaders   Dennis Le Boeuf/Liming Jing
Illustrator   Nan Jun/Jessie Willcox Smith

WORDS
800

MP3

Let's Enjoy Masterpieces!

All the beautiful fairy tales and masterpieces that you have encountered during your childhood remain as warm memories in your adulthood. This time, let's indulge in the world of masterpieces through English. You can enjoy the depth and beauty of original works, which you can't enjoy through Chinese translations.

The stories are easy for you to understand because of your familiarity with them. When you enjoy reading, your ability to understand English will also rapidly improve.

This series of *Let's Enjoy Masterpieces* is a special reading comprehension booster program, devised to improve reading comprehension for beginners whose command of English is not satisfactory, or who are elementary, middle, and high school students. With this program, you can enjoy reading masterpieces in English with fun and efficiency.

This carefully planned program is composed of 5 levels, from the beginner level of 350 words to the intermediate and advanced levels of 1,000 words. With this program's level-by-level system, you are able to read famous texts in English and to savor the true pleasure of the world's language.

The program is well conceived, composed of reader-friendly explanations of English expressions and grammar, quizzes to help the student learn vocabulary and understand the meaning of the texts, and fabulous illustrations that adorn every page. In addition, with our "Guide to Listening," not only is reading comprehension enhanced but also listening comprehension skills are highlighted.

In the audio recording of the book, texts are vividly read by professional American actors. The texts are rewritten, according to the levels of the readers by an expert editorial staff of native speakers, on the basis of standard American English with the ministry of education recommended vocabulary. Therefore, it will be of great help even for all the students that want to learn English.

Please indulge yourself in the fun of reading and listening to English through *Let's Enjoy Masterpieces*.

約翰娜・施皮里

Johanna Spyri
(1827–1901)

Johanna Spyri, the author of *Heidi*, was born on June 12, 1827, in the village of Hirzel, seven miles from Zurich, Switzerland. Her father was a doctor, and she had five other siblings.

She spent most of her childhood helping to tend goats and sometimes take care of her father's patients. In 1852 she married lawyer Bernhard Spyri and moved to Zurich. There, she began writing children's stories. The motive of her writing was simply to make money to help wounded refugees who came home from the Franco-Prussian war.

Her first novel *A Leaf on Vrony's Grave* was published in 1871. *Heidi*, her masterpiece, was published in 1880, and it became an immediate success. This children's novel was later translated into about 50 languages.

Before she died in 1901, she wrote nearly 50 different children's novels, some of which also were translated and introduced to countries worldwide. Nevertheless, *Heidi* proved to be the most popular, successful, and remembered classic throughout her entire writing career. It has appeared in print, in film, and on television all over the world.

About the story

At the age of five, Heidi was taken to live with her short-tempered and hermit-like grandfather in the Swiss mountains. With her cheerful and high-spirited nature, Heidi quickly won the heart of the aloof old man. She grew fond of her new mountain life with Grandfather and befriended with goatherd Peter and his grandmother.

However, two years later, Heidi was taken away again, this time, to a rich family in Frankfurt. She was to be the playmate to the rich family's wheelchair-ridden daughter, Clara.

Though she brought just as much joy to Clara as she did to others, she missed her family and friends in the Swiss Alps and wished to return home.

When her wish was finally granted, it seemed like a miracle to Heidi. And when Clara came to visit Heidi the next year, Clara experienced a miracle as well.

HOW TO USE THIS BOOK

本書使用說明

① Original English texts

It is easy to understand the meaning of the text, because the text is divided phrase by phrase and sentence by sentence.

② Explanation of the vocabulary

The words and expressions that include vocabulary above the elementary level are clearly defined.

③ Response notes

Spaces are included in the book so you can take notes about what you don't understand or what you want to remember.

④ Check Up

Review quizzes to check your understanding of the text.

∩ *Audio Recording*

In the audio recording, native speakers narrate the texts in standard American English. By combining the written words and the audio recording, you can listen to English with great ease.

Audio books have been popular in Britain and America for many decades. They allow the listener to experience the proper word pronunciation and sentence intonation that add important meaning and drama to spoken English. Students will benefit from listening to the recording twenty or more times.

After you are familiar with the text and recording, listen once more with your eyes closed to check your listening comprehension. Finally, after you can listen with your eyes closed and understand every word and every sentence, you are then ready to mimic the native speaker.

Then you should make a recording by reading the text yourself. Then play both recordings to compare your oral skills with those of a native speaker.

HOW TO IMPROVE READING ABILITY
如何增進英文閱讀能力

① Catch key words

Read the key words in the sentences and practice catching the gist of the meaning of the sentence. You might question how working with a few important words could enhance your reading ability. However, it's quite effective. If you continue to use this method, you will find out that the key words and your knowledge of people and situations enables you to understand the sentence.

② Divide long sentences

Read in chunks of meaning, dividing sentences into meaningful chunks of information. In the book, chunks are arranged in sentences according to meaning. If you consider the sentences backwards or grammatically, your reading speed will be slow and you will find it difficult to listen to English.

You are ready to move to a more sophisticated level of comprehension when you find that narrowly focusing on chunks is irritating. Instead of considering the chunks, you will make it a habit to read the sentence from the beginning to the end to figure out the meaning of the whole.

③ Make inferences and assumptions

Making inferences and assumptions is part of your ability. If you don't know, try to guess the meaning of the words. Although you don't know all the words in context, don't go straight to the dictionary. Developing an ability to make inferences in the context is important.

The first way to figure out the meaning of a word is from its context. If you cannot make head or tail out of the meaning of a word, look at what comes before or after it. Ask yourself what can happen in such a situation. Make your best guess as to the word's meaning. Then check the explanations of the word in the book or look up the word in a dictionary.

④ Read a lot and reread the same book many times

There is no shortcut to mastering English. Only if you do a lot of reading will you make your way to the summit. Read fun and easy books with an average of less than one new word per page. Try to immerse yourself in English as often as you can.

Spend time "swimming" in English. Language learning research has shown that immersing yourself in English will help you improve your English, even though you may not be aware of what you're learning.

CONTENTS

Introduction 4

How to Use This Book 6

How to Improve Reading Ability 8

Chapter 1

Uncle Alp 14

Chapter 2

At Grandfather's 20

Chapter 3

Out With Peter and the Goats 26

Chapter 4

A Visit to Grannie 32

Chapter 5

Leaving the Alps 38

Chapter 6

In Frankfurt 42

Chapter 7

Mr. Sesemann and Grandmamma 50

Chapter 8

Homesickness 57

Chapter 9

Clara's Visit 66

Chapter 10

Clara Walked! 72

Chapter 11

The Miracle 78

Appendixes

❶ Guide to Listening Comprehension 86

❷ Exercise 90

Translation 97

Answers 124

Before You Read

Heidi

Heidi was a cheerful five-year-old orphan. She enjoyed tending goats and living with her Grandfather in a mountain village in Switzerland.

Detie

Detie was Heidi's aunt. She had taken care of Heidi since her parents' death.

Uncle Alp

Uncle Alp was Heidi's grandfather. He was known for his bad temper. People in his village didn't like him, so he led a reclusive life in a hut on the mountain. Though grumpy, patriarchal, and strict, he was also very kind.

Peter

Peter was a goatherd. He tended goats for the villagers.

Grannie

Grannie was Peter's grandmother.
She enjoyed talking to Heidi.

Mr. Sesemann

Mr. Sesemann was a rich businessman in Frankfurt. He was often away from home on business trips.

Clara

Clara was Mr. Sesemann's daughter.
She was sick and confined to a wheelchair.

Miss Rottenmeier

Miss Rottenmeier was the Sesemanns' housekeeper. She looked after Clara.

Grandmamma

Grandmamma was Clara's grandmother.
She encouraged Heidi to learn to read.

· Chapter One ·

 Uncle Alp

One sunny morning in June, a young woman, Detie, was on the way up the Swiss Alps with her niece, Heidi. Heidi's parents died five years ago. Since then, Detie had looked after Heidi.

Recently, Detie found employment[1] as a housekeeper in a rich family in Frankfurt, the industrial[2] and cultural capital of Germany. She could no longer take care of Heidi. Thus, Detie was taking Heidi to Uncle Alp, Heidi's grandfather.

1. **employment** [ɪmˋplɔɪmənt] (n.) 工作；受僱

2. **industrial** [ɪnˋdʌstriəl] (a.) 工業的

Detie met a village woman on the way, and they started talking. Heidi stood by her aunt and felt bored. She saw a young boy nearby and then went over to talk to him. The boy, named Peter, was a goatherd[3] for the villagers.

It was a hot sticky[4] day. Heidi obviously[5] wore too much clothes. Indeed, her cheeks were as red as apples. She took off some clothes and left them on the ground.

After a while, Aunt Detie went looking for Heidi. She saw Heidi wearing only her undershirt and petticoat[6].

Check Up Choose the correct answer.

_____ 1. How was the weather that morning in June?
Ⓐ It was sandy. Ⓑ It was nuclear. Ⓒ It was clear.

_____ 2. What's Detie's relationship to Heidi?
Ⓐ She was Heidi's grandmother.
Ⓑ She was Heidi's aunt.
Ⓒ She was Heidi's mother.

Ⓣ Ⓕ 3. Heidi gave Grannie a gift before they parted.

Ans: C, B, F

3. **goatherd** [ˋgoʊthɜːrd] (n.) 牧山羊人

4. **sticky** [ˋstɪki] (a.) 濕黏的

5. **obviously** [ˋɑːbviəsli] (adv.) 顯然地

6. **petticoat** [ˋpetikoʊt] (n.) 襯裙

"Where are your clothes?" asked Detie angrily.

The girl pointed down the mountain and replied "over there."

Detie offered Peter a penny as a commission[1] to retrieve[2] Heidi's clothes, because going down the hill again would be a heavy tax[3] on her strength.

Then Detie and Heidi were on the road again, together with Peter and his goats. Before long, they came to a lonely hut on the top of the mountain. On a wooden bench in front of the hut was Heidi's grandfather.

The villagers referred[4] to him as Uncle Alp, who was seen as a strange old man and well known for his bad temper. Nobody knew much about his background. They only knew about the accidental death of his son, Heidi's father.

His death came to Heidi's mother as a shock. She soon got a fever and died a few weeks later. After the death of his son and daughter-in-law, the old man lived alone on the mountain.

Heidi was happy to see her grandfather. She greeted warmly, "Hello, Grandfather!"

---

1. **commission** [kə`mɪʃən] (n.) 佣金
2. **retrieve** [rɪ`triːv] (v.) 收回
3. **tax** [tæks] (n.) 負擔；壓力
4. **refer** [rɪ`fɜːr] (v.) 談及

Looking annoyed, the old man shouted, "Who are you?"

"She's your granddaughter, Uncle. You might not recognize[5] Heidi. She is five years old and has come here to live with you," Detie responded.

Heidi greeted warmly, "Hello, Grandfather!"

Uncle Alp didn't seem to care about her response and turned to shout at Peter, "Get out of here with the goats, Peter. Take mine with you!"

Peter obeyed[6] immediately and quickly disappeared.

"It's your turn to take care of her now, Uncle," Detie continued. "I have looked after her since she was an infant.

"No, that's not right! What can I do with her? She'll miss you and cry and cry," said Uncle Alp angrily.

Check Up Choose the correct answer.

T
F
4. Uncle Alp's background was largely unknown to the villagers.

Ans: T

5. **recognize** [ˋrɛkəgnaɪz] (v.) 認識;認出

6. **obey** [oʋˋbeɪ] (v.) 聽從;服從

17

"She is not my responsibility anymore. I have done my duty, and now it is time for you to do yours."

The old man stood up, raised his arms in the air, and threatened[1], "Get out of here immediately! Don't you ever come back again!"

"Goodbye to you then, and to you too, Heidi," Detie called as she backed away and hurried down the mountain.

Detie was sorry about Heidi, but she had no options[2]. She had to leave for Frankfurt today. It was impossible for her to take a child to work. She was extremely[3] happy about the well-paid job. For this, she couldn't help but smile.

✔ *Check Up* Choose the correct answer.

_____ 5. How old was Heidi when she was taken to live with her grandfather?
   A She was five years old.
   B She was four years old.
   C She was seven years old.

T F 6. Uncle Alp was fairly happy to see Detie and Heidi.

T F 7. Detie supposed that Uncle Alp remembered Heidi.

T F 8. Detie eventually left Heidi behind and went down the mountain alone.

Ans: A, F, F, T

---

1. **threaten** ['θretən] (v.) 威脅
2. **option** ['ɑːpʃən] (n.) 選擇

3. **extremely** [ɪk'striːmli] (adv.) 極度地

Chapter Two

At Grandfather's

Detie was gone. There were only Heidi and Uncle Alp. Heidi was very curious about her grandfather's hut[1].

"I want to look around your house, Grandfather," said Heidi.

"Come in, then. Bring your clothes with you."

"I don't need them. I want to run about like the goats."

"All right, but bring them anyway. We'll put them in the cupboard[2]."

Heidi followed Uncle Alp into the house.

There was a table and some chairs by one wall. In one corner, there lay a bed for Uncle Alp. There was also a fireplace across the room. The grandfather opened the cupboard. Heidi then put away her clothes behind her grandfather's.

1. **hut** [hʌt] (n.) 小屋

2. **cupboard** [ˋkʌbərd] (n.) 櫥櫃

"Where do I sleep, Grandfather?" Heidi asked.

"Wherever you like," the old man replied.

Heidi looked around and saw a ladder beside her grandfather's bed. She climbed it and found herself in a loft[3]. There was a large quantity[4] of fresh hay in the loft. Through a small window, she could look down into the valley.

"I want to sleep here!" she said. Uncle Alp then gave her the sheet and cover and helped make a bed comfortable to sleep in.

"What a wonderful bed I have! If only it were bedtime now," exclaimed[5] Heidi.

"Let's have lunch first," said Uncle Alp.

✓ *Check Up* Choose the correct answer.

_____ 1. Despite her unwillingness, Heidi put away her clothes _____.
　Ⓐ in the cupboard
　Ⓑ on the table
　Ⓒ on her grandfather's bed

_____ 2. What exactly was Heidi's bed made of?
　Ⓐ Wood.
　Ⓑ Iron.
　Ⓒ Fresh hay.

Ans: A, C

3. **loft** [lɑːft] (n.) 閣樓
4. **quantity** [ˋkwɑːntəti] (n.) 數量

5. **exclaim** [ɪkˋskleɪm] (v.) 驚呼

The old man came down the ladder and walked to the fireplace. He stuck a piece of cheese on a fork and moved it to and fro over the fire. Meantime, Heidi was busy setting the table.

"Very good! I am glad you can do some work," said Uncle Alp.

Pretty soon the cheese turned golden. The grandfather gave Heidi a slice[1] of cheese, a large proportion[2] of bread, and a bowl of milk.

"It's the best meal ever!" Heidi exclaimed.

After lunch Uncle Alp needed to do some chores[3]. They both went to the goat shed[4]. There, Heidi watched Uncle Alp work.

After some time, Uncle Alp decided to make a comfortable chair for Heidi, because the chairs by the table were way too short for her.

Check Up Choose the correct answer.

T
F
3. Heidi had cheese, bread, milk, and a variety of other food for dinner.

Ans: F

1. **slice** [slaɪs] (n.) 薄片
2. **proportion** [prəˈpɔːrʃən] (n.) 部分
3. **chores** [tʃɔːrz] (n.) (pl.) 家務
4. **shed** [ʃed] (n.) 棚子

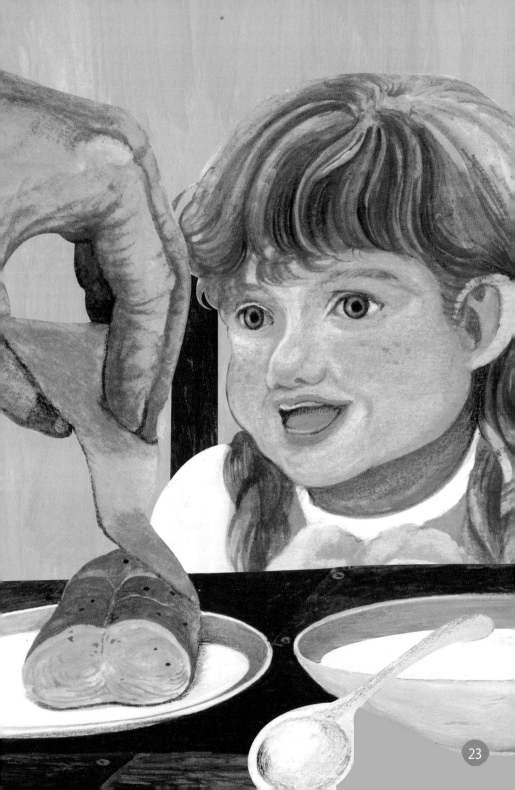

Uncle Alp was a fast worker. It didn't take him long to finish making the chair. His skills in carpentry[1] amazed Heidi.

"A chair for me! How fast you made it!" the girl exclaimed.

When the evening came, a whistle attracted Heidi's attention. She saw Peter and the goats in a column[2] of files[3]. She was very happy and ran to greet them.

After a while, they came near the hut. A white goat and a brown one emerged[4] from the herd[5] and approached[6] Uncle Alp.

It wasn't difficult to tell the two goats apart because of their distinct[7] colors. Still, Heidi wanted to know their names.

"Are they ours, Grandfather?"

"Yes, the white goat is called Daisy, and the brown one Dusky," stated[8] Uncle Alp.

Uncle Alp led the goats to the goat shed. Then he took Heidi inside for dinner.

That night Heidi slept comfortably and soundly[9] in her cozy[10] loft.

 Check Up Choose the correct answer.

T
F
4. Uncle Alp made a high chair for Heidi to demonstrate his carpentry technique.

Ans: F

---

1. **carpentry** [ˋkɑːrpɪntri] (n.) 木工
2. **column** [ˋkɑːləm] (n.) 縱隊
3. **file** [faɪl] (n.) 縱列
4. **emerge** [ɪˋmɜːrdʒ] (v.) 出現
5. **herd** [hɜːrd] (n.) 牧群
6. **approach** [əˋproutʃ] (v.) 靠近
7. **distinct** [dɪˋstɪŋkt] (adj.) 清楚的
8. **state** [steɪt] (v.) 說
9. **soundly** [ˋsaundli] (adv.) 酣然地
10. **cozy** [ˋkouzi] (a.) 舒適的

Chapter Three

⚆ Out With Peter and the Goats

The next morning Heidi awoke and heard her grandfather talking to Peter. She got out of her bed to join them.

"Do you want to go to the pasture[1] with Peter?" the grandfather asked.

Heidi was overjoyed[2] to hear that and cried, "I'd love to!"

Peter had a bag, which was filled with his meal. Uncle Alp put bread, a slice of cheese, and a bowl in the bag for Heidi. Peter looked at Heidi's lunch with eyes wide open. The food for Heidi was twice as big as his normal meal!

"You should milk from the goats two bowls of milk for Heidi at noon," demanded[3] Uncle Alp. "Make sure she doesn't fall over the cliffs[4]."

Shortly, the two children reached the pasture. "Here we are. I mainly spend my day tending[5] the herd here," observed[6] Peter.

He sat down on the grass and put his bag aside. He then began to nap[7], and Heidi played quietly with the goats.

About noon Peter began to prepare lunch. Heidi looked at Peter's meal. It was relatively small. She kindly shared her bread and cheese with Peter.

✓ Check Up Choose the correct answer.

_____1. What did Uncle Alp ask Peter to do for Heidi particularly at noon?
   Ⓐ To take Heidi back home.
   Ⓑ To get two bowls of milk from the goats for Heidi.
   Ⓒ To share Heidi's bread and cheese.

_____ 2. At lunch, what did Heidi give Peter?
   Ⓐ A loan.   Ⓑ A bag.   Ⓒ Bread and cheese.

Ans: B, C

---

1. **pasture** [ˋpæstʃər] (n.) 牧草地
2. **overjoyed** [ˌouvərˋdʒɔɪd] (adj.) 欣喜若狂的
3. **demand** [dɪˋmænd] (v.) 要求
4. **cliff** [klɪf] (n.) 懸崖
5. **tend** [tend] (v.) 照料；管理
6. **observe** [əbˋzɜːrv] (v.) 說
7. **nap** [næp] (v.) 睡午覺

Peter was surprised at the little girl's kindness and nodded his thanks to Heidi. For him, it was the biggest meal ever.

Suddenly, Peter jumped to his feet and ran. A goat was apparently[1] about to fall over the cliff. Peter pulled the goat back to the field.

Angry at the goat, he reached out one hand in an attempt[2] to pick up a stick on the ground. He was about to beat the goat. Heidi certainly didn't want the poor animal to suffer[3] from Peter's beating. So, she begged Peter not to punish the goat.

"I will let him go, but you have to give me a slice of cheese again tomorrow," said Peter.

"OK, you can have my cheese tomorrow," ensured[4] Heidi.

"It's a deal." Peter released[5] the goat.

---

1. **apparently** [ə`pærəntli] (adv.) 顯然地
2. **attempt** [ə`tempt] (v.) 企圖
3. **suffer** [`sʌfər] (v.) 遭受
4. **ensure** [ɪn`ʃur] (v.) 保證
5. **release** [rɪ`liːs] (v.) 釋放

As the day passed, the sun was sinking out of sight behind the mountains. The appearance of the world seemed to vary[1] with the setting sun. Everything seemed to be red with flame[2]. To Heidi, the redness looked almost like a world on fire.

"Look, everything is on fire!" Heidi exclaimed.

"It is not really fire," explained Peter. He then told her that it was like that most days.

Now it was time to go home. Heidi and Peter took the same route[3] back to Uncle Alp's hut. Heidi had enjoyed a great day.

She told her grandfather all the interesting things about the day. That night she even dreamed of goats jumping in the pasture.

1. **vary** [`veri] (v.) 變化
2. **flame** [fleɪm] (n.) 火焰
3. **route** [ruːt] (n.) 路線

✓ Check Up Choose the correct answer.

_____ 3. What did Peter plan to do when the goat was pulled back to the field?
Ⓐ To bind the goat to a stake.
Ⓑ To beat on the goat.
Ⓒ To push the goat over the cliffs.

Ⓣ Ⓕ 4. Peter wouldn't spare the goat unless Heidi promised to give him milk tomorrow as an exchange.

Ⓣ Ⓕ 5. Heidi was involved in a fire accident.

Ans: B, F, F

31

◦ Chapter Four ◦

 A Visit to Grannie

Day after day, Heidi went to the pasture with Peter until the fall came. The fall wind on the mountain could be very strong and might blow little Heidi off the cliffs. At the thought of such a risk, Uncle Alp asked Heidi to stay home.

Heidi enjoyed staying home to watch Grandfather make round goat cheese and fix things with the hammer and nails. She really admired Grandfather's technical skills. The weather was getting increasingly cold, and pretty soon the winter came.

One snowy day, when Heidi and her grandfather were at lunch, Peter showed up with lots of snow on his clothes. He quickly said hi and ran straight to the stove[1] to warm himself up. At the sight of this, Heidi laughed.

Peter didn't need to herd[2] goats in the winter. Instead, he went to school on weekdays. Today there was no school, so Peter came over to see Heidi. He stayed in the hut that afternoon. Before leaving, Peter invited Heidi to visit him sometime.

"Grannie would love to meet you," he said.

The concept[3] of such a visit thrilled[4] Heidi tremendously[5].

Check Up Choose the correct answer.

T F 1. Heidi helped Uncle Alp make round goat cheese.

T F 2. Peter started schooling because of the improvement of his family's financial circumstances.

T F 3. Heidi asked Peter to extend her greetings to his grandmother.

Ans: F, F, F

---

1. **stove** [stoʊv] (n.) 暖爐
2. **herd** [hɜːrd] (v.) 放牧
3. **concept** [ˋkɑːnsept] (n.) 想法；概念
4. **thrill** [θrɪl] (v.) 使……興奮
5. **tremendously** [trɪˋmendəsli] (adv.) 非常地

In the following days, Heidi couldn't resist[1] the enticing[2] idea of visiting Peter's family and kept asking her grandpa to take her to meet Grannie.

"I must go today; otherwise, Grannie will be tired of waiting," said Heidi one day.

Uncle Alp went up to the loft to fetch a thick blanket. "Come on, then," he said.

They went outdoors together. Uncle Alp dragged out a big sledge[3] and sat on it. He then wrapped[4] Heidi up in the blanket and held her in one arm. He pushed off the sledge with both feet, and they skidded[5] down the mountain.

The sledge moved so fast that Heidi screamed with joy. She felt as if she were flying through the air like a bird.

Soon they arrived at Grannie's hut. Uncle Alp asked her to go into the hut and come back home before it grew dark. Then he left and went up the mountain.

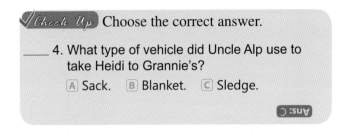

Check Up Choose the correct answer.

_____ 4. What type of vehicle did Uncle Alp use to take Heidi to Grannie's?
Ⓐ Sack.　Ⓑ Blanket.　Ⓒ Sledge.

Ans: C

1. **resist** [rɪˋzɪst] (v.) 抵抗
2. **enticing** [ɪnˋtaɪsɪŋ] (a.) 誘人的
3. **sledge** [slɛdʒ] (n.) 雪橇
4. **wrap** [ræp] (v.) 包裹
5. **skid** [skɪd] (v.) 滑行

⌂12

Heidi entered the hut. She saw an old woman, spinning. Heidi was sure this was Peter's grandmother. She went up to the old woman and introduced herself, "How do you do, Grannie? I'm Heidi."

Grannie sought[1] for Heidi's hand and held it in her own. "Are you the little girl with Uncle Alp?"

"Yes, I am." Heidi then looked around the house and found the shutter[2] loose. She told Grannie to look at the shutter.

"I am blind," revealed[3] the old woman.

Heidi was shocked and felt deeply sorry for Grannie. She started crying out loud, "Is there anyone who can make it light for you again?" Heidi kept on sobbing[4].

"Don't cry, my child. Tell me, how do you like it here so far?" said Grannie.

Heidi dried her tears and detailed[5] to Grannie about her life with her grandfather. That day they had a great time talking to each other.

1. **seek** [siːk] (v.) 尋找
   (seek-sought-sought)
2. **shutter** [ˈʃʌtər] (n.) 百葉窗
3. **reveal** [rɪˈviːl] (v.) 揭露
4. **sob** [sɑːb] (v.) 哭泣
5. **detail** [ˈdɪteɪl] (v.) 詳述
6. **situation** [ˌsɪtʃuˈeɪʃən] (n.) 處境；狀況

The next day Heidi and her grandfather came to Grannie's hut to help fix the shutter.

"My grandfather will fix the shutter for you," Heidi explained the situation[6] to Grannie.

Uncle Alp first examined the shutter, and then he fixed it.

Heidi continued to visit Grannie almost every day. The two had grown very fond of each other.

"Thank the Lord! It's the child again," Grannie exclaimed whenever she heard Heidi's footsteps.

Check Up Choose the correct answer.

_____ 5. What type of housing did Grannie live in?

Ⓐ Hut.　Ⓑ Studio.　Ⓒ Apartment.

_____ 6. What was Heidi's reaction when she learned that Peter's grandmother couldn't see?

Ⓐ She felt angry.

Ⓑ She felt surprised and sad.

Ⓒ She felt homesick.

Ans: A, B

Chapter Five

🎧13 Leaving the Alps

Two winters passed. One day Aunt Detie showed up unexpectedly. To Heidi's astonishment[1], Aunt Detie came to take her away. Uncle Alp didn't want Heidi to leave him. The two adults had an argument.

"Heidi is eight years old and still can't read. I will take her to live with a wealthy family in Frankfurt."

"Shut up!" the grandfather roared[2].

"The family has a lame[3] daughter. Heidi can be her playmate and learn how to read."

"Are you finished?" Uncle Alp wasn't even interested in Detie's explanation.

"This kind of chance doesn't come every day," said Aunt Detie.

---

1. **astonishment** [əˋstɑːnɪʃmənt] (n.) 驚訝
2. **roar** [rɔːr] (v.) 怒吼
3. **lame** [leɪm] (a.) 瘸腿的

"Fine! Take her and spoil her," Uncle Alp warned and left angrily.

"You made Grandfather angry," said Heidi.

"He'll be fine," sighed[1] Aunt Detie.

Heidi didn't really want to go, but Aunt Detie promised to take her back again soon. So, they started down the mountain. On their way, they met Peter.

"Where are you going?" asked Peter.

"I am going to Frankfurt. I must say goodbye to Grannie."

"There is no time for that," Detie pulled Heidi away and hurried on.

Peter rushed home. "She's taking Heidi away."

"Who's taking my child away?" asked Grannie anxiously[2].

Grannie didn't wait for Peter's answer. She opened the window and called, "Heidi!"

"That was Grannie. I must see her and say goodbye," said Heidi.

"We need to hurry to the railway station. You can bring her a gift later," said Detie.

"What should I bring her?"

"Some soft white rolls[3], maybe. The black bread might be too hard for her."

---

1. **sigh** [saɪ] (v.) 嘆氣
2. **anxiously** [ˋæŋkʃəslɪ] (adv.) 焦急地
3. **roll** [roʊl] (n.) 麵包捲
4. **resident** [ˋrezɪdənt] (n.) 居民

Heidi was gone. Uncle Alp looked angrier than before. Most of the residents[4] in the village were more afraid of him than ever.

However, Grannie would always tell people about Uncle Alp's kindness to Heidi and about his help with the shutter. Both of them missed Heidi very much.

✓ *Check Up* Choose the correct answer.

T F 1. Aunt Detie intended to take Heidi away.

_____ 2. Under Detie's arrangement for Heidi, Heidi would stay _____ in Frankfurt.
  Ⓐ in a rich community   Ⓑ with her lame daughter
  Ⓒ with a rich family

_____ 3. How would you define Uncle Alp's attitude with Detie?
  Ⓐ Highly understanding.   Ⓑ Argumentative.   Ⓒ Proper.

_____ 4. On their way down the mountain, Detie and Heidi bumped into _____.
  Ⓐ Peter.   Ⓑ Grannie.   Ⓒ Detie's employer.

T F 5. Heidi gave Grannie a gift before they parted.

Ans: T, C, B, A, F

41

Chapter Six

🎧15 In Frankfurt

The wealthy family in Frankfurt lived in a big house. The house belonged to Mr. Sesemann. His wife died years ago, and his daughter, Clara, was sick and had to sit in a wheelchair.

Mr. Sesemann was often far away on business. So, Mr. Sesemann left the management and administration[1] of the house to Miss Rottenmeier. She was then the head of the housekeeping staff[2] and managed every aspect of the internal[3] household affairs.

Her strict requirements[4] for everything made her colleagues all afraid of her. She was sort of an authority[5] figure in the house.

Upon Detie and Heidi's arrival, Miss Rottenmeier wasn't happy. First, Clara was four years older than Heidi, but Miss Rottenmeier had specifically mentioned finding a 12-year-old girl like Clara.

She was also surprised at Heidi's incapability[6] in reading. To Miss Rottenmeier, Heidi was certainly below Clara's level.

Check Up Choose the correct answer.

_____ 1. What was Mr. Sesemann's job?
  A He was an agent in a travel agency.
  B He was a software engineer in the information technology sector.
  C He was a businessman.

_____ 2. How was Clara's physical condition?
  A Healthy.　B Sick.　C Blind.

Ans: C, B

4. **requirement** [rɪˋkwaɪrmənt] (n.) 規定

1. **administration** [ədˏmɪmɪˋstreɪʃən] (n.) 行政；管理

5. **authority** [əˋθɔːrɪti] (n.) 當權者

2. **staff** [stæf] (n.) 員工

3. **internal** [ɪnˋtɜːrnəl] (a.) 內部的

6. **incapability** [ˏɪnkeɪpəˋbɪlɪti] (n.) 無能

"Where did you find this girl, from an outlying[1] district[2]?" Miss Rottenmeier groaned[3]. She wanted to replace Heidi with a suitable candidate[4], but Detie just made an excuse and quickly left the house.

Miss Rottenmeier was puzzled[5] for a moment, and then she ran after Detie. It was too late. Detie was gone.

Heidi remained by the door. Clara had looked on during the interview, and now she said to Heidi, "Come here, Heidi. Do you like Frankfurt?"

"No. I will go home tomorrow, and bring Grannie some soft white rolls."

"You are a funny girl. You are here to keep me company. We will study together, and you can learn to read from Mr. Usher. It will be fun."

That evening Miss Rottenmeier lectured[6] Heidi about appropriate[7] manners and behavior in the house. Heidi could hardly pay attention to the lengthy[8] explanation of rules and regulations[9].

She was only interested in the white rolls on the dinner table. She secretly put some in her pocket.

"Grannie would be happy!" she thought.

✓ *Check Up* Choose the correct answer.

_____ 3. Which of the following is NOT in the agreement between Detie and Miss Rottenmeirer?
  Ⓐ The girl must be two years older than Clara.
  Ⓑ The girl should be literate.
  Ⓒ The girl must be suitable for Clara.

_____ 4. Mr. Usher was a _____.
  Ⓐ consumer   Ⓑ tutor   Ⓒ client

Ⓣ Ⓕ 5. Heidi ate all the white rolls at the dinner table.

Ans: A, B, F.

---

1. **outlying** [`aʊt͵laɪŋ] (a.) 偏遠的
2. **district** [`dɪstrɪkt] (n.) 地區
3. **groan** [ɡroʊn] (v.) 抱怨
4. **candidate** [`kændɪdeɪt] (n.) 人選
5. **puzzled** [`pʌzəld] (a.) 困惑的
6. **lecture** [`lɛktʃər] (v.) 訓斥

7. **appropriate** [ə`proʊprɪət] (a.) 恰當的;適當的
8. **lengthy** [`lɛŋθi] (adj.) 冗長的
9. **regulation** [͵rɛɡjʊ`leɪʃən] (n.) 規則;規定

The next morning Heidi woke up but couldn't remember her whereabouts[1] at first. Everything around her was so strange, but soon she remembered all the happenings the day before.

She attempted to open the window to feel the sunshine, but it was too high for her. She felt disappointed and confined[2]. She missed her mountain home.

Every morning Heidi and Clara took lessons together from Mr. Usher. He taught Heidi the alphabet. Even after several sessions[3] about the letters, Heidi still couldn't learn all of them. They were too complex[4] for her.

In the afternoon, Clara usually rested. Heidi could do anything as long as she stayed out of trouble.

1. **whereabouts** [ˋwɛrəˋbaʊts]
   (n.) 所在的地方
2. **confined** [kənˋfaɪnd]
   (a.) 監禁的
3. **session** [ˋsɛʃən] (n.) 講習課
4. **complex** [ˌkɑːmˋplɛks]
   (a.) 複雜難懂的

47

In the evening, Heidi would tell Clara about her life on the mountain. The more Heidi talked about the Alps, the more fondness[1] she felt of everything in those distant mountains.

"I must go home tomorrow," Heidi claimed constantly[2]. Nevertheless, Clara always brought her relief[3] with soothing words. The growing stock[4] of white rolls for Grannie also kept Heidi staying.

At times Heidi's will[5] to go home was too great to bear. Once she packed all her belongings and decided to leave. Then she ran into Miss Rottenmeier at the door.

Miss Rottenmeier knew about Heidi's intention and was angry. "It was not very civil[6] of you to run away like this! You are a thankless child," scolded Miss Rottenmeier.

---

1. **fondness** [ˈfɑːndnəs] (n.) 喜愛
2. **constantly** [ˈkɑːnstəntli] (adv.) 時常地
3. **relief** [rɪˈliːf] (n.) 安慰
4. **stock** [stɑːk] (n.) 累積
5. **will** [wɪl] (n.) 意念；意願

As a consequence[7], Heidi remained. That night at the dinner table, Miss Rottenmeier watched Heidi constantly, but nothing mischievous[8] happened. Heidi hardly touched her food except for the white rolls.

Check Up Choose the correct answer.

T F 6. The possibility of obtaining more white rolls made Heidi willing to stay.

T F 7. Heidi wanted to leave the house because she was afraid of Clara's disease.

Ans: T, F

6. **civil** [`sɪvəl] (a.) 有禮貌的

7. **consequence** [`kɑːnsɪkwəns] (n.) 結果

8. **mischievous** [`mɪstʃɪvəs] (a.) 調皮的

Chapter Seven

🎧19 Mr. Sesemann and Grandmamma

One day Mr. Sesemann came home from business. He didn't wait for the servants to settle[1] his luggage but went directly to Clara's room.

Clara loved her father dearly and was very excited to see him. They greeted and kissed each other. Meanwhile, Heidi stood shyly in one corner.

"You must be our little Swiss girl. Come here. Are you two good friends already?" Mr. Sesemann asked.

"Yes, Clara is very nice to me," Heidi replied.

In the evening, Miss Rottenmeier gave Mr. Sesemann a detailed account[2] of Heidi's rustic[3] behavior, but Mr. Sesemann didn't see a need to make a fuss[4] about it. Miss Rottenmeier wasn't pleased, but she could only obey Mr. Sesemann's directives.

Check Up Choose the correct answer.

T F 1. Mr. Sesemann and Clara greeted each other in the presence of Heidi.

_____ 2. Miss Rottenmeier complained to Mr. Sesemann about Heidi's _____.
   A behavior
   B relations with Clara
   C reading capability

Ans: 1. A

1. **settle** [ˋsetl] (v.) 安放；安置
2. **account** [əˋkaʊnt] (n.) 說明
3. **rustic** [ˋrʌstɪk] (a.) 粗俗的
4. **fuss** [fʌs] (n.) 小題大作

20

Two weeks later Mr. Sesemann left, and Clara's grandmother came for a visit. Before the grandmother's visit, Heidi heard many stories about the old lady. Clara normally called her grandmother "Grandmamma." So, Heidi called her Grandmamma, too.

Grandmamma was a kind and loving lady. With her amicable[1] approach to children, a close friendship was soon established[2] between her and Heidi.

One afternoon Grandmamma showed Heidi a large storybook with an exhibition[3] of various regional[4] landscapes. In the book, Heidi found references[5] to her mountain life, including a picture of a goatherd and goats in a green pasture. Heidi looked at the picture and cried.

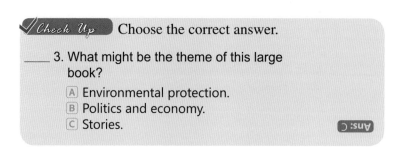

> ✓ *Check Up* Choose the correct answer.
>
> _____ 3. What might be the theme of this large book?
> 　Ⓐ Environmental protection.
> 　Ⓑ Politics and economy.
> 　Ⓒ Stories.
> 　　　　　　　　　　　　　Ans: C

1. **amicable** [ˋæmɪkəbəl]
   (a.) 友善的
2. **establish** [əˋstæblɪʃ] (v.) 建立
3. **exhibition** [ˌɛksɪˋbɪʃən]
   (n.) 展示
4. **regional** [ˋriːdʒənəl]
   (a.) 地區的
5. **reference** [ˋrɛfərəns] (n.) 提及

21

Grandmamma knew about Heidi's problem. To encourage her, Grandmamma promised to give her the book as an award[1], but she had to learn to read first.

Heidi nodded, though she wasn't sure about the idea. She thought of Peter's struggle[2] with reading, and now she could relate[3] to that.

Grandmamma asked Heidi to trust herself, for many children at Heidi's age could learn to read without any significant[4] difficulty.

Heidi nodded again but still sobbed on. She couldn't confide in Grandmamma about her wish to return home. She remembered Miss Rottenmeier's words vividly: only an unthankful child ran away.

"My dear child, sometimes you seem sorrowful," said Grandmamma. "You probably don't want other people to know your sorrows, but you can always pray to God. You don't have to be religious[5]. God will give you happiness and joy."

A week later, Mr. Usher told Grandmamma about Heidi's performance on reading.

"The investment[6] of my time and effort in her training proved worthwhile! In contrast[7] to the past, she is a much better reader now!" exclaimed Mr. Usher with confidence[8].

Of course, it wasn't just Mr. Usher's training. Grandmamma should also take the credit[9], for her strategy[10] of promising an award propelled[11] Heidi to keep learning.

Check Up Choose the correct answer.

[T] [F] 4. With regard to the difficulty of reading, Heidi seemed to identify with Peter.

[T] [F] 5. According to Grandmamma's advice, Heidi could always go to church and talk to the minister there.

Ans: T, F

1. **award** [ə`wɔːrd] (n.) 獎品
2. **struggle** [`strʌgəl] (n.) 奮鬥
3. **relate** [rɪ`leɪt] (v.) 産生共鳴
4. **significant** [sɪg`nɪfɪkənt] (a.) 重大的
5. **religious** [rɪ`lɪdʒəs] (a.) 虔誠的
6. **investment** [ɪn`vestmənt] (n.) 投入
7. **contrast** [`kɑːntræst] (n.) 對比
8. **confidence** [`kɑːnfɪdəns] (n.) 信心
9. **credit** [`kredɪt] (n.) 功勞
10. **strategy** [`strætədʒi] (n.) 策略
11. **propel** [prə`pel] (v.) 激勵

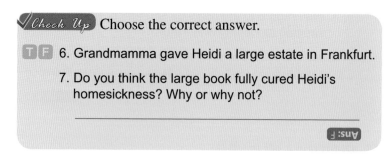

22   Still, Grandmamma was excited to hear that statement from Mr. Usher. That night, as per[1] Grandmamma's promise, Heidi was awarded the large book.

"It's yours now," said Grandmamma.

The book became Heidi's greatest property[2]. She loved the pictures in the book and made practical[3] application[4] of her reading skills. She would read the stories in the book to Clara and Grandmamma.

Pretty soon Grandmamma's visit ended, and it was spring again. Heidi looked melancholic[5].

"Peter must be on the pasture with the goats now," she thought to herself.

The more she thought of things back home, the more her homesickness grew.

Check Up Choose the correct answer.

T F 6. Grandmamma gave Heidi a large estate in Frankfurt.

7. Do you think the large book fully cured Heidi's homesickness? Why or why not?

_____

Ans: F

---

1. **per** [pər] (prep.) 按照
2. **property** [ˈprɑːpərti] (n.) 財產
3. **practical** [ˈpræktɪkəl] (a.) 實際的
4. **application** [ˌæplɪˈkeɪʃən] (n.) 運用
5. **melancholic** [ˈmelənˌkɑːlɪk] (a.) 憂鬱的；憂傷的

Homesickness

One morning something strange happened in the Sesemanns' residence[1]. The servants found the front door open. No one admitted leaving the door open. Strangely enough, nothing was stolen in the house.

In the following mornings, the servants repetitively found the door open.

One night two servants decided to stand watch. Around midnight a strange noise came from the outside of the servants' room. They rushed out and saw a white form on the stairs.

They wanted to take a good look at it, but it was gone in a moment. They were scared.

1. **residence** [ˈrezɪdəns] (n.) 住宅

24

The servants reported to Miss Rottenmeier about their findings the previous night. They had no evidence[1], but they made a connection between the white form and a ghost.

In shock, Miss Rottenmeier wrote a letter and made an appeal[2] to Mr. Sesemann to come home immediately for the security[3] of the house.

Mr. Sesemann didn't believe in the existence[4] of ghosts and could only laugh at the servants' associations[5]. Still, he returned home several days later.

He poked fun at[6] Miss Rottenmeier's timidity[7] and overreaction, but he promised to stay up to meet the "ghost" himself.

It was awfully quiet that night. Around midnight, Mr. Sesemann suddenly heard something. He went out and saw a white figure.

1. **evidence** [ˋevɪdəns] (n.) 證據
2. **appeal** [əˋpiːl] (n.) 請求
3. **security** [sɪˋkjurɪtɪ] (n.) 安全
4. **existence** [ɪgˋzɪstəns] (n.) 存在
5. **association** [ə͵souʃiˋeɪʃən] (n.) 聯想
6. **poke fun at** . . . 揶揄……
7. **timidity** [tɪˋmɪdɪti] (n.) 膽小
8. **figure** [ˋfɪgjər] (n.) 人影
9. **soothingly** [ˋsuːðɪŋli] (adv.) 安慰地
10. **primary** [ˋpraɪmeri] (a.) 主要的
11. **scheme** [skiːm] (n.) 陰謀

"Who is it?" he shouted.

The figure[8] turned around and screamed. Mr. Sesemann looked at the figure's face and was surprised. It was Heidi in her white nightgown.

"Why are you here, child?"

"I . . . I don't know," Heidi stumbled.

"Come here. We should talk," said Mr. Sesemann soothingly[9].

Through the conversation, Mr. Sesemann finally understood Heidi's primary[10] problem. It wasn't Heidi's wicked scheme[11] for running away. In actual fact, Heidi was simply homesick.

Check Up Choose the correct answer.

T F 1. The two servants had conflicting versions of what they saw around midnight.

_____ 2. What was the specific reason for Heidi's sleepwalking during the night?
Ⓐ Her homesickness.
Ⓑ Her wage.
Ⓒ Her difficulty in learning to read.

Ans: F, A

25

She dreamed of everyone and everything back home every night. The impact[1] of the homesickness made her walk in her sleep.

The next day Mr. Sesemann granted[2] Heidi's wish to go home. Of course, Clara had everything to say in opposition[3] to this.

She tried to prevent[4] her father from following through his decision, but through communication, her father convinced her.

"This is possibly best for Heidi. We shouldn't be selfish," said Mr. Sesemann. "I'll let you visit Heidi next year."

Clara packed lots of stuff[5] in a basket for Heidi. The basket also contained a considerable[6] amount of white rolls.

---

1. **impact** [ˈɪmpækt] (n.) 影響
2. **grant** [grænt] (v.) 同意
3. **opposition** [ˌɑːpəˈzɪʃən] (n.) 反對
4. **prevent** [prɪˈvent] (v.) 阻止
5. **stuff** [stʌf] (n.) 物品
6. **considerable** [kənˈsɪdərəbəl] (a.) 相當多的

Meanwhile, Aunt Detie arrived. She was appointed[7] to accompany[8] Heidi back to Switzerland. Heidi was very happy, and she said her thanks and goodbye to Clara and Mr. Sesemann and left.

Heidi was thrilled to be back to the Swiss Alps again. She dropped by Peter's house and saw Grannie inside.

Grannie heard the door open and said, "Oh, Heidi used to make an entry[9] like that."

Check Up Choose the correct answer.

_____ 3. Clara gave Heidi a basket, and it included lots of stuff such as _____.
Ⓐ Sack.   Ⓑ Blanket.   Ⓒ Sledge.

Ans: C

7. **appoint** [ə`pɔɪnt] (v.) 指派
8. **accompany** [ə`kʌmpəni] (v.) 陪同
9. **entry** [`entri] (n.) 進入

"Grannie! I am back!"

"Oh, thank the Lord[1]! It is you. You're back!" said Grannie in tears.

"Don't cry, Grannie. I got you some white rolls. You don't have to eat hard black bread anymore." Heidi laid the white rolls in Grannie's lap.

"Oh, child. You are such a blessing[2] to me," exclaimed Grannie in a transport[3] of delight[4].

Heidi took Grannie's hand and said, "I must go to Grandfather now, but I'll come back tomorrow."

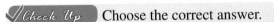

Choose the correct answer.

T F 4. Besides giving Grannie the white rolls, Heidi also made an equal distribution of the white rolls among the villagers.

Ans: F

1. **Lord** [lɔːrd]
   (n.) (大寫) 上帝，基督
2. **blessing** [ˋblɛsɪŋ] (n.) 賜福

3. **transport** [ˋtrænspɔːrt]
   (n.) 欣喜若狂
4. **delight** [ˋdɪˋlaɪt] (n.) 愉快

After climbing the old familiar path, Heidi saw Grandfather outside the hut. She ran to him and threw her arms around him tight.

She shouted happily, "Grandfather! Grandfather! Grandfather!"
"So, you're back, huh?" said Grandfather.

Grandfather gave her a bowl of milk. Heidi drank with the utmost[1] content[2] and exclaimed, "Our milk is the best, Grandfather!"

Heidi had often dreamed of this day while in Frankfurt, and now her dream became a reality[3]. She was happy, and so was Grandfather.

That night Grandfather went up to the loft about ten times to see Heidi in her sleep.

---

1. **utmost** [`ʌtmoust] (a.) 最大的
2. **content** [`kɑːntent] (n.) 滿足
3. **reality** [ri`ælɪti] (n.) 事實；現實

Chapter Nine

🎧 Clara's Visit

After Heidi left, Clara and Heidi often sent their greetings to each other through mail. In her letters, Clara promised to visit Heidi the following spring.

Heidi really looked forward to seeing Clara again. She wanted to show Clara around her hometown. The winter seemed so long, and Heidi got tired of waiting at times. Fortunately, several things kept her busy.

First, she had to attend school. She also often visited Grannie and read to her. Heidi's reading capability[1] marveled[2] Grannie a lot.

Besides, under Heidi's guidance, Peter performed better in class. By the end of winter, Peter could read texts[3] of some simple hymns[4].

Spring finally came. Everything on the Alps looked lush[5] green. One day Peter brought Heidi a letter.

"It was from Clara! She will come here soon!" Heidi read with excitement.

Upon hearing that, Peter felt jealous. He turned away and slammed[6] the door with a bang[7] behind him.

1. **capability** [ˌkeɪpəˈbɪləti] (n.) 能力
2. **marvel** [ˈmɑːrvəl] (v.) 感到驚訝
3. **text** [tekst] (n.) 文本
4. **hymn** [hɪm] (n.) 聖歌
5. **lush** [lʌʃ] (a.) 青翠繁茂的
6. **slam** [slæm] (v.) 猛力關上
7. **bang** [bæŋ] (n.) 砰一聲

Check Up Choose the correct answer.

_____ 1. How did Heidi and Clara manage to keep in touch with each other?

Ⓐ By phone.
Ⓑ By email.
Ⓒ By mail.

Ans: C

On the day of Clara's visit, Heidi saw a procession[1] of visitors on the mountain trail. Clara was sitting in a sedan[2] chair carried by two men. Then she saw Grandmamma on the horseback, and a young fellow carried Clara's wheelchair. Finally, there's a porter with a load of covers and furs[3].

"Here they come!" shouted Heidi, jumping up and down with joy.

Soon the visitors arrived by the hut. The girls greeted each other joyfully. Grandmamma got down off the horse and greeted Uncle Alp.

Then she greeted Heidi, "How well you look, Heidi!"

Grandfather lifted Clara from the litter[4] and into her wheelchair. Heidi then pushed Clara around to see the goat shed, the fir[5] trees, and fully blossomed meadows.

1. **procession** [prə`seʃən] (n.) 行列；隊伍
2. **sedan** [sɪ`dæn] (n.) 轎子
3. **fur** [fɜːr] (n.) 毛皮
4. **litter** [`lɪtər] (n.) 轎
5. **fir** [fɜːr] (n.) 冷杉
6. **occasion** [ə`keɪʒən] (n.) 時機
7. **benefit** [`benɪfɪt] (n.) 益處
8. **hurray** [hu`reɪ] (int.) 好耶

"How beautiful it is, Heidi," cried Clara.

"But these are nothing," Heidi said. "It is more beautiful up there, where the goats are feeding."

At lunch Clara exclaimed, "Everything tastes so much better here."

Uncle Alp seized the occasion[6] and said to Grandmamma, "We would love to have Clara stay with us for the summer. The mountain air would be a great benefit[7] for her."

"Oh, my dear uncle," said Grandmamma, "that idea just came across my mind. I can't thank you enough."

"Hurray[8]!" the two girls yelled.

Around dusk Grandmamma left with the porters. Uncle Alp made a bed for Clara next to Heidi's. She also had a perfect view of the mountains and the starry skies through the round window.

Check Up Choose the correct answer.

_____ 2. Heidi pushed Clara in her wheelchair to see the natural _____ in the Alps.

A features   B resources   C development

T F 3. Grandmamma was slightly opposed to Uncle Alp's proposal to have Clara stay for the summer.

Ans: A, F

69

Every day a series of excursions[1] awaited Heidi and Clara. Heidi would push Clara around to pick flowers. They'd also chitchat[2] or write letters to Grandmamma.

Clara got to know Peter as well. However, Peter considered Clara as a threat. To him, it seemed like a competition with Clara for Heidi's affection[3].

Generally, Peter was a boy with an even[4] disposition[5], but this time, his rage[6] and jealousy simply grew unbearable.

Once, in an access[7] of fury[8], he shook Clara's wheelchair with both fists and ran away.

That didn't help remove or even reduce his anger much. He was still angry and missed his companion dearly.

4. What did Peter's jealousy and rage arise from?

_____

1. **excursion** [ɪkˋskɜːrʒən] (n.) 遠足
2. **chitchat** [ˋtʃɪt͵tʃæt] (v.) 閒聊
3. **affection** [əˋfekʃən] (n.) 鍾愛
4. **even** [ˋiːvən] (adj.) 同樣的

5. **disposition** [͵dɪspəˋzɪʃən] (n.) 性情
6. **rage** [reɪdʒ] (n.) 怒火
7. **access** [ˋækses] (n.) 爆發
8. **fury** [ˋfjʊri] (n.) 暴怒

Chapter Ten

🎧 31 Clara Walked!

"How I want to go up the mountain to see the pasture[1]! If only I could walk," said Clara one morning.

"You look stronger now, Clara. Will you try, just once, to stand on the ground?" asked Uncle Alp.

"I'm not one hundred percent sure. It'll hurt," said Clara.

"Just try. I will hold you," assured[2] Uncle Alp.

Clara held on to Uncle Alp's arm and pulled herself up from the chair. During the process, Clara trembled[3] a bit and lost her balance several times. Still, she made it. Without a cane or any sort of equipment[4], she could stand erect[5] on the ground now.

"Great job, Clara!" Heidi screamed happily.

The next morning Peter passed Uncle Alp's hut without blowing his whistle. He quietly moved toward Uncle Alp's goat shed, but the first thing in sight was Clara's wheelchair.

Peter's anger steamed to the boiling point. He came to the wheelchair and impulsively[6] gave it a hard push. The wheelchair began rolling crazily down the mountain, and within a blink[7] of an eye, it disappeared over the edge.

Then, out of guilt[8], Peter rushed up the mountain without Uncle Alp's goats.

Check Up Choose the correct answer.

_____ 1. Uncle Alp thought perhaps Clara could spend a day on the pasture because _____.
  Ⓐ Clara had potential
  Ⓑ Clara seemed stronger now
  Ⓒ a research on handicapped kids said so

Ⓣ Ⓕ 2. The wheelchair fell a victim to Peter's anger at Clara.

Ans: B, T

1. **pasture** [`pæstʃər] (n.) 牧草地
2. **assure** [ə`ʃur] (v.) 保證
3. **tremble** [`trembəl] (v.) 顫抖
4. **equipment** [ɪ`kwɪpmənt] (n.) 器具
5. **erect** [ɪ`rekt] (adj.) 直挺的
6. **impulsively** [ɪm`pʌlsɪvli] (adv.) 衝動地
7. **blink** [blɪŋk] (n.) 一瞥
8. **guilt** [gɪlt] (n.) 內疚

32

A few minutes later, Heidi came out of the hut.

"Where is the wheelchair?" asked Heidi.

"Where's Peter? The goats are still in the shed," said Uncle Alp angrily.

"Oh, no. I'll never see the pasture without my wheelchair," said Clara in grief[1].

"Don't worry. I'll carry you up," said Uncle Alp.

The three of them reached the pasture and saw Peter with the goats there.

Uncle Alp asked Peter about the wheelchair, but Peter claimed, "What wheelchair? I don't know."

Uncle Alp said no more. He gave the girls their lunch bags and left.

Heidi and Clara sat on the ground to appreciate[2] the beauty around them. On a whim[3], Heidi suggested, "Let me carry you to a beautiful site."

"It's impossible, Heidi. You are smaller than I." Clara hesitated.

Heidi asked Peter to help, but Peter was reluctant[4]. So, Heidi threatened, "Come over here this instant, or you'll be sorry."

Upon hearing that, Peter's guilt of destroying[5] Clara's wheelchair made him obey Heidi's order.

At first, Clara was scared. Then she stood up and tried to step forward. She felt hurt and cried. However, she labored[6] on and took additional[7] steps.

For Clara, learning to walk was like a battle[8], but she decided to make a commitment[9]. She committed herself to walking on her own to appreciate her friends' kindness and encouragement.

"Good! Do it again. Just concentrate[10] and follow my lead," Heidi urged.

1. **grief** [griːf] (n.) 傷心
2. **appreciate** [əˋpriːʃieɪt] (v.) 欣賞
3. **whim** [wɪm] (n.) 念頭
4. **reluctant** [rɪˋlʌktənt] (a.) 不情願的
5. **destroy** [dɪˋstrɔɪ] (v.) 破壞
6. **labor** [ˋlebər] (v.) 努力前進
7. **additional** [əˋdɪʃənəl] (a.) 額外的
8. **battle** [ˋbætəl] (n.) 戰役
9. **commitment** [kəˋmɪtmənt] (n.) 承諾
10. **concentrate** [ˋkɑːnsəntreɪt] (v.) 全神貫注

33

Clara took another step, and then another and another. Finally, Heidi and Peter let go of Clara.

"Oh, Heidi, See! I can walk now!" Clara hollered[1] with joy and in tears.

With Clara's gradually steady footsteps, they finally reached the blossomed spot and spent the rest of the day there.

Several days passed, and Clara's trembling steps became increasingly steady. Every day she found it easier and was able to go a longer distance[2].

She decided to surprise her grandmother with her wonderful news, for Grandmamma would come in a few days to take Clara home.

✓ *Check Up* Choose the correct answer.

T F 3. Clara was in tears twice. The former tears were brought about because of pain; the latter because of joy.

Ans: T

---

1. **holler** [ˋhɑːlər] (v.) 大聲呼喊   2. **distance** [ˋdɪstəns] (n.) 距離

Chapter Eleven

The Miracle

On the morning of Grandmamma's visit, Clara and Heidi sat on the bench to wait for her. Upon Grandmamma's arrival, Clara held Heidi's arm and stood up.

The two girls began walking toward Grandmamma. At first, Grandmamma was shocked, for the Clara in front of her wasn't the original[1] Clara.

Grandmamma began laughing and crying. She ran toward the girls and hugged first Clara and then Heidi, and then Clara again, unable to speak for joy.

Finally Grandmamma exclaimed, "Thank the Lord! This is a miracle!"

✓ Check Up Choose the correct answer.

_____ 1. What was the essential factor that made Grandmamma laugh and cry?

Ⓐ She's crazy.　　Ⓑ Clara could walk.
Ⓒ Uncle Alp and Heidi's contribution to Clara's health.

Ans: B

---

1. **original** [ə`rɪdɪnəl] (a.) 原本的

35

Grandmamma then said to Uncle Alp, "My dear uncle! How can we thank you enough! This is all your work and care without any medical[1] treatment[2] or facility[3]!"

"It was the sunshine and mountain air," Uncle Alp said with a smile.

"Yes, and also our goats' milk," Heidi added.

Meanwhile, Peter approached with an obvious expression[4] of horror and guilt. He said to Grandmamma, "I am sorry! And now, it's all broken into pieces."

"What's wrong with the child?" said Grandmamma in confusion.

"I guess," said Uncle Alp, "he is responsible for Clara's missing wheelchair."

Grandmamma finally understood the context[5] of Peter's words and said, "Everyone should be punished for a wicked deed, but this one turned to good. Peter's behavior enabled[6] Clara to walk."

Now, Peter, promise me. You will reflect[7] on your mistake and always think twice to avoid doing something wicked."

Peter nodded and promised to reform[8].

"Here, I want you to remember the people from Frankfurt." Grandmamma gave Peter a dollar.

Peter couldn't believe his eyes. He got a payment instead of a punishment.

Check Up Choose the correct answer.

T F 2. Like Grandmamma, Uncle Alp was also confused by Peter's description about Clara's missing wheelchair.

Ans: F

1. **medical** [ˋmedɪkəl]
   (a.) 醫療的
2. **treatment** [ˋtriːtmənt]
   (n.) 治療
3. **facility** [fəˋsɪləti]
   (n.) 設備；工具
4. **expression** [ɪkˋspreʃən]
   (n.) 表情
5. **context** [ˋkɑːntekst]
   (n.) 來龍去脈
6. **enable** [ɪˋneɪbəl]
   (v.) 使……能夠
7. **reflect** [rɪˋflekt] (v.) 反省
8. **reform** [rɪˋfɔːrm] (v.) 改過
   自新

36

"How about you, Heidi? What would you like for a present?" asked Grandmamma gracefully.

With little consideration[1], Heidi said, "A bed like mine in Frankfurt for Grannie. That way, she won't have to sleep in a cold, hard bed again."

"A first-rate mattress[2] will be sent immediately upon my arrival in Frankfurt," Grandmamma promised.

The carriage[3] for Grandmamma and Clara was waiting at the foot of the mountain. Uncle Alp carried Clara down, for she couldn't risk[4] walking the long mountain trail[5].

1. **consideration**
   [kənˌsɪdəˈreɪʃən] (n.) 考慮
2. **mattress** [ˈmætrɪs]
   (n.) 床墊
3. **carriage** [ˈkærɪdʒ]
   (n.) 馬車
4. **risk** [rɪsk] (v.) 冒險
5. **trail** [treɪl] (n.) 小路

Clara was sad about leaving, but she promised to come again next summer.

"Summer will come again soon," said Heidi. "We can go up to the pasture together again. It will be great!"

Heidi and Uncle Alp watched the carriage leave. Heidi ran after the carriage and shouted, "See you next summer, Clara!"

✓*Check Up* Choose the correct answer.

_____ 3. Clara promised Heidi to visit her _____.
  Ⓐ the following summer
  Ⓑ on an annual basis
  Ⓒ if the profit of her father's business was good enough to afford such a visit

Ans: A

Appendixes

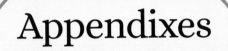 Guide to Listening
   Comprehension
 Exercise

Guide to Listening Comprehension

When listening to the story, use some of the techniques shown below. If you take time to study some phonetic characteristics of English, listening will be easier.

Get in the flow of English.

English creates a rhythm formed by combinations of strong and weak stress intonations. Each word has its particular stress that combines with other words to form the overall pattern of stress or rhythm in a particular sentence.

When you are speaking and listening to English, it is essential to get in the flow of the rhythm of English. It takes a lot of practice to get used to such a rhythm. So, you need to start by identifying the stressed syllable in a word.

Listen for the strongly stressed words and phrases.

In English, key words and phrases that are essential to the meaning of a sentence are stressed louder. Therefore, pay attention to the words stressed with a higher pitch. When listening to an English recording for the first time, what matters most is to listen for a general understanding of what you hear. Do not try to hear every single word. Most of the unstressed words are articles or auxiliary verbs, which don't play an important role in the general context. At this level, you can ignore them.

Pay attention to liaisons.

In reading English, words are written with a space between them. There isn't such an obvious guide when it comes to listening to English. In oral English, there are many cases when the sounds of words are linked with adjacent words.

For instance, let's think about the phrase "**take off**," which can be used in "take off your clothes." "Take off your clothes" doesn't sound like [teɪk ɔːf] with each of the words completely and clearly separated from the others. Instead, it sounds as if almost all the words in context are slurred together, [ˈteɪkɔːf], for a more natural sound.

Shadow the voice of the native speaker.

Finally, you need to mimic the voice of the native speaker. Once you are sure you know how to pronounce all the words in a sentence, try to repeat them like an echo. Listen to the book again, but this time you should try a fun exercise while listening to the English.

This exercise is called "shadowing." The word "shadow" means a dark shade that is formed on a surface. When used as a verb, the word refers to the action of following someone or something like a shadow. In this exercise, pretend you are a parrot and try to shadow the voice of the native speaker.

Try to mimic the reader's voice by speaking at the same speed, with the same strong and weak stresses on words, and pausing or stopping at the same points.

Experts have already proven this technique to be effective. If you practice this shadowing exercise, your English speaking and listening skills will improve by leaps and bounds. While shadowing the native speaker, don't forget to pay attention to the meaning of each phrase and sentence.

Listen to what you want to shadow many times. Start out by just trying to shadow a few words or a sentence.

 Mimic the CD out loud. You can shadow everything the speaker says as if you are singing a round, or you also can speak simultaneously with the recorded voice of the native speaker.

 As you practice more, try to shadow more. For instance, shadow a whole sentence or paragraph instead of just a few words.

2   Exercise

A   Multiple Choice.

_____ ❶ Why did Aunt Detie take Heidi to live with Uncle Alp?

(a) There was a great economic turmoil in the country.

(b) She was out of budget for raising Heidi.

(c) She had to go to Frankfurt to work and therefore couldn't take care of Heidi anymore.

_____ ❷ Peter was a professional _____, for he _____ goats for a living.

(a) herd goat, tended

(b) goatherd, tended

(c) herdgoat, tended

_____ ❸ The sex of Uncle Alp's goats could be inferred from the story: they were female. What is the most likely scenario for such inference?

(a) According to Heidi, their goats' milk made Clara stronger.

(b) Uncle Alp once taught Heidi to distinguish the sexual characteristics of male and female goats.

(c) Most farmers in Switzerland only raise female goats.

_____ ④ Aunt Detie came back to the Alps and took Heidi away to _____.

(a) attend a labor union's conference in Frankfurt

(b) work for a rich institution in Frankfurt

(c) live with a wealthy family in Frankfurt

_____ ⑤ Ms. Rottenmeier's status in the Sesemanns' residence is similar to that of a/an _____ in a commercial setting.

(a) accountant

(b) chief executive

(c) insurance agent

_____ ⑥ Mr. Sesemann was a _____.

(a) rich man often on business

(b) rich councilor of the Frankfurt city council

(c) rich campaign activist in the parliament

_____ ⑦ Two servants saw a _____ around midnight and mistook it for a ghost.

(a) white form

(b) white roll

(c) white committee member

_____ ⑧ Under Heidi's guidance, Peter could _____.

    (a) be an author

    (b) write hymns

    (c) read sentences of some simple hymns

_____ ⑨ Grandmamma forgave Peter and gave him

    a _____.

    (a) fund

    (b) scholarship

    (c) dollar

B Put the following procedures in correct orders.

❶ He then wrapped Heidi up in the blanket and held her in one arm.

❷ Uncle Alp dragged out a big sledge and sat on it.

❸ He pushed off the sledge with both feet, and they skidded down the mountain.

❹ Soon they arrived at Grannie's hut.

_____ ⇨ _____ ⇨ _____ ⇨ _____

C Fill in the Blanks.

Complete the following excerpts from the story with the words given.

> responsibility   cry   turn

"It's your ① _____ to take care of her now, Uncle," Detie said.

"Yeah, right! What can I do with her? She'd ② _____ for you," said Uncle Alp angrily.

"She is not my ③ _____ ."

> deal   slice   ensured   released

"I will let him go, but you have to give me a ④ _____ of cheese again tomorrow," said Peter.

"OK, you can have my cheese tomorrow," ⑤ _____ Heidi.

"It's a ⑥ _____ ." Peter ⑦ _____ the goat.

over	at	to	on
about	up	in	

Suddenly, Peter jumped ⑧ _____ his feet and ran. A goat was apparently ⑨ _____ to fall ⑩ _____ the cliff. He was very angry ⑪ _____ the goat, so he reached one hand out ⑫ _____ an attempt to pick ⑬ _____ a stick ⑭ _____ the ground.

popularity	passed away	opposing
awfully	situation	

❶ The two political parties have ⑮ _____ views on the country's future.

❷ Jennifer's husband ⑯ _____ two years ago. Now she is a working mom with four children to take care of.

❸ Paul's plan sounded perfect in theory but worked ⑰ _____ in practice.

❹ The writer's latest novel was published last week and soon obtained great ⑱ _____ .

❺ John always makes a thorough analysis of a ⑲ _____ before coming to a conclusion.

D Rewrite the order of words provided.

Rottenmeier / findings / reported / servants / Miss /
The / night / the / about / to / previous / their

_____

_____

Translation

　　《海蒂：阿爾卑斯山的少女》的作者約翰娜・施皮里（Johanna Spyri, 1827–1901），於西元 1827 年 6 月 12 日出生於瑞士蘇黎世七哩外的希瑟爾村，家裡有五位兄弟姊妹，父親是一位醫生。

　　她童年時常幫忙看顧羊群，偶爾也會幫忙父親照顧病人。1852 年，她與律師伯納・施皮里結婚，並搬到蘇黎世，開始了童書寫作生涯，而她寫作賺錢的目的，只是為了幫助那些從普法戰爭歸來的傷兵難民。

　　她的首部小說《芙隆尼墳上的一片葉子》（*A Leaf on Vrony's Grave*）於 1871 年出版，而大作《海蒂：阿爾卑斯山的小女孩》（*Heidi*）則於 1880 年出版，並立即獲得廣大迴響，此本兒童小說後來譯有近 50 種語言。

　　她在 1901 年辭世之前，創作各種兒童小說近 50 本，有幾部作品被翻譯成各種語言，在世界各地出版，不過她的寫作生涯還是以《海蒂：阿爾卑斯山的小女孩》一書最成功，予人深刻印象且為人熟知，不管是全球各地的書籍或影視都可見其蹤跡。

　　海蒂在五歲時就被帶到瑞士山上，與易怒孤僻的爺爺一同居住。她開朗勇敢的個性很快就融化了爺爺冷漠的心，也越來越喜歡跟爺爺住在山上，還有和牧童彼得與其奶奶交朋友的全新生活。

　　然而兩年後，海蒂又被帶走了，這次是到法蘭克福的有錢人家裡去，當坐輪椅上的富家小姐克萊拉的玩伴。

　　雖然她為克萊拉帶來許多樂趣，就如同她帶給其他人的一樣，但她好想念瑞士阿爾卑斯山上的家人與朋友，期盼能回到家中。

　　就像是奇蹟似地，她的願望成真了。而隔年克萊拉來訪，也歷經了奇蹟般的境遇。

角色介紹

Heidi 海蒂
一位性情開朗的五歲孤女，與爺爺一起住在瑞士山上的小村中，樂於看顧羊群。

Detie 蒂堤
海蒂的阿姨，自海蒂的雙親去世後便負責照顧她。

Uncle Alp 阿爾卑斯伯伯
海蒂的爺爺，由於脾氣很壞，村中的人都不喜歡他，所以在山中小屋過著離群索居的生活。雖然性情乖戾、古怪又嚴苛，其實還是個善良的好人。

Peter 彼得
為村民牧羊的牧童。

Grannie 婆婆
彼得的奶奶，很喜歡跟海蒂聊天。

Mr. Sesemann 謝斯曼先生
法蘭克福的富商，常因工作出差而不在家。

Clara 克萊拉
謝斯曼先生的掌上明珠，因生病而長期坐輪椅。

Miss Rottenmeier 洛頓梅爾小姐
謝斯曼家的管家，負責照顧克萊拉。

Grandmamma 奶奶
克萊拉的奶奶，鼓勵海蒂唸書。

[第 一 章] 阿爾卑斯伯伯

p. 14–15 在天氣和煦的六月早晨，一位年輕女子蒂堤正帶著姪女海蒂前往阿爾卑斯山，海蒂的雙親在五年前去世，自那時起，蒂堤便一直照顧著她。

但最近蒂堤在德國的工業與文化重鎮法蘭克福的富有人家那邊覓得一份管家的工作，沒辦法再顧著海蒂了，所以得帶她到阿爾卑斯伯伯，也就是她爺爺那邊去。

蒂堤在路上遇見一名村婦，開始聊了起來，站在一旁的海蒂覺得無聊，看見附近有位男孩，便走向前去攀談，男孩叫彼得，是幫村民牧羊的牧童。

天氣又濕又熱，海蒂顯然是穿了太多，臉頰紅得還真像顆蘋果，她便脫下幾件衣服，丟到地上。過了一會兒，蒂堤阿姨過來找她，卻發現她只穿著內衣和襯裙。

p. 16–17 蒂堤氣極敗壞地問：「妳的衣服呢？」

她指著山下一處回答：「在那裡。」

但跑下山丘實在太累人了，蒂堤便給彼得一分錢當作跑腿費，去將海蒂的衣物拿來。

蒂堤與海蒂再次上路，彼得與羊群一同隨行。不久他們走到山頂的一間偏僻小屋，海蒂的爺爺就坐在屋前的木凳上。

村民都叫他阿爾卑斯伯伯，被認為是個古怪老人，還有讓人不敢領教的壞脾氣。除了他兒子，也就是海蒂父親意外去世的這件事以外，其他人對他的背景一無所知。

海蒂父親的死，對海蒂母親是一個很大的打擊，母親不久後發高燒，幾個禮拜後也跟著離開人世了。自從兒子跟媳婦相繼去世後，老人就獨自住在山中。

海蒂很開心見到爺爺，熱情地向他打招呼：「爺爺您好啊！」

臉色不悅的老人大聲地說：「妳是誰？」

「伯伯，你或許不認得她，但她可是您的孫女，已經五歲囉，要搬來跟你住呢。」蒂堤回答。

阿爾卑斯伯伯不理會她說什麼，便轉向彼得大吼：「彼得，帶著羊群滾出這裡，連我的羊也一塊帶走！」

彼得立刻照辦，一溜煙離開了。

「現在換你照顧她了，伯伯。」蒂堤接著說：「我已經從她嬰孩時就照顧她了。」

阿爾卑斯伯伯氣憤地說：「這樣不對！她會想妳而哭鬧不休，那我要拿她怎麼辦？」

p. 18「她已經跟我沒關係了。我已盡到責任，是該換你了。」

老人起身，抬起雙臂在空中揮舞並威脅著說：「立刻給我滾！再也不准出現在我面前！」

蒂堤後退著說：「那就再見啦，海蒂妳也是。」便匆匆離開山上。

她對海蒂感到抱歉，但她今天一定要前往法蘭克福，所以實在是無計可施了。她總不可能帶著孩子工作吧，想到工作的優厚酬勞，她不禁揚起笑意。

［第二章］在爺爺家

p. 20-21 蒂堤走後，只剩海蒂與阿爾卑斯伯伯了。她對爺爺的小屋感到非常好奇。

　　海蒂説：「我想參觀你的屋子，爺爺。」

　　「那就進來吧，帶著妳的衣服。」

　　「我才不需要衣服呢，我想像山羊一樣到處跑來跑去。」

　　「好，不過還是拿進來放在櫥櫃裡吧。」

　　海蒂便跟著爺爺進屋去了。

　　牆邊有張桌子和幾張椅子，角落放了張阿爾卑斯伯伯的床，而屋子對邊則有個壁爐。爺爺打開壁爐後，海蒂將衣物收好放在爺爺衣服的後面。

　　海蒂詢問：「那我要睡哪裡？」

　　「哪裡都行。」老人回答。

　　她環視四周，看見爺爺床邊有張梯子，便爬了上去，到了閣樓裡。裡頭有好多新鮮乾草，透過一扇小窗，還可以俯視山谷呢。

　　「我就睡這！」她説。阿爾卑斯伯伯拿了床單跟被子給她，還替她整理出個舒服的床好讓她睡。

　　「我有一個好舒服的床喔！真希望睡覺時間到了。」海蒂興奮地嚷嚷。

　　阿爾卑斯伯伯説：「我們先吃午餐吧。」

p. 22 老人下了樓梯，走向壁爐，用叉子串了一塊起士在火上來回地燒烤，同時海蒂則是忙著擺餐具。

「很好！我很高興妳也能幹些活。」他説。

起司一下就烤成金黃色了，爺爺給她一片起司、一大塊麵包跟一碗牛奶。

海蒂大喊：「這可真是最棒的大餐呢！」

午飯過後，阿爾卑斯伯伯要幹活，他們一起走到羊舍，海蒂就看著他做事。

過了一會兒，阿爾卑斯伯伯決定要替她造張舒適的椅子，因為桌旁的椅子對海蒂來説實在是太矮了。

p. 24–25 阿爾卑斯伯伯動作很快，完成一張椅子並不費什麼時間，海蒂對他的木工功力可真是讚賞不已。

「給我的椅子啊！你做得可真快耶！」小女孩驚呼。

傍晚時分，一聲口哨引起海蒂的注意，她看見彼得領著結成縱隊的山羊，便很高興地跑去迎接他。

過了一會兒，他們走到了小屋附近，牧群中的有隻白色與棕色的山羊走近了阿爾卑斯伯伯。

要辨認兩隻毛色相差甚多的山羊一點都不難，不過海蒂還是想知道牠們叫什麼名字。

「爺爺，牠們是我們的羊嗎？」

「是呀。白色那隻叫戴西；棕色的叫道斯奇。」阿爾卑斯伯伯説。

他將羊帶到羊舍後，就跟海蒂到屋內用晚餐。

那晚，海蒂在她舒適的閣樓裡睡得又香又甜。

[第三章] 與彼得和羊群出門去

p. 26–27 隔天海蒂醒來，聽見爺爺在和彼得講話，便起身下床，加入他們的談話。

爺爺問：「妳想跟彼得去牧草地嗎？」

海蒂聽到他這樣說非常開心地大聲回答：「好啊！」

彼得帶了個裝著餐點的袋子，阿爾卑斯伯伯則是替海蒂準備了個袋子，裡頭放有麵包、一片起司和一個碗。彼得眼睛瞪得大大地看著海蒂的午餐，她的食物足足有他平常分量的兩倍呢！

阿爾卑斯爺爺命令地說：「你中午要擠兩碗山羊奶給海蒂喝，還要顧好她，別讓她跌到山下去了。」

兩個小鬼頭不到一會兒就到達牧草地了，彼得說：「我們到啦，我平常白天都在這裡看顧羊群。」

彼得一屁股在草地上坐了下來，把袋子放到一旁，便開始打盹，而海蒂則靜靜地跟羊群玩耍。

快接近中午時，彼得開始準備午餐。海蒂看到他的午餐跟自己的比起來，還真少了許多，便貼心地與彼得分享麵包與起司。

p. 28 彼得對這位小女孩的善良感到訝異，連忙對她點頭道謝，對他而言，今天這一餐是他有史以來最豐盛的一餐。

忽然間，彼得整個人突然跳了起來，有隻山羊似乎就快掉到懸崖下了，他趕緊將羊拉回草地。

怒氣沖沖的彼得伸出手拿起地上的木條，正要鞭打羊隻時，海蒂懇求他不要處罰羊隻，她可不希望這可憐的小東西遭到鞭打。

「我可以放過牠，可是妳明天得再給我一片起司。」彼得說。

海蒂信誓旦旦地說：「好，明天我的分給你。」

「那就說定了。」彼得便放了羊。

p. 30–31 白晝過去，太陽下山，萬物景象隨著日落而變化萬千，萬物似乎都閃耀著紅色光芒。海蒂覺得這片紅通通的景象就如同世界在燃燒一樣。

「你看，所有東西都在燃燒呢！」海蒂驚呼。

彼得解釋：「那才不是火。」告訴她平常就是這幅景象。

到了該回家的時間了，他們倆循原路回到了阿爾卑斯伯伯的小屋。海蒂過了很棒的一天。

她告訴爺爺有關白天所發生的趣事，當晚還夢見羊隻們在草地上蹦蹦跳跳呢。

[第四章] 拜訪婆婆

p. 32–33 秋天來臨前，海蒂每天都和彼得一起到草原上。山上的秋風強勁，是有可能把小海蒂吹下山崖的。阿爾卑斯伯伯顧慮到此風險，便要海蒂待在家裡。

海蒂享受待在家中，看著爺爺製作羊酪，用鐵鎚與釘子修理物品的生活。她真的是很佩服爺爺的專業技術。天氣漸漸轉涼，冬天很快就來了。

一個下雪天，海蒂與爺爺正在用午餐時，彼得滿身是雪的出現在她家。他迅速打了聲招呼便直接衝向火爐好暖暖身子，海蒂看到此景不禁笑了出來。

冬季時，彼得平日就不用看顧羊群，而是去上學，但今天不用上課，他就來探望海蒂。那天下午就留在小屋中，要離開前，彼得邀請海蒂改天去他家坐坐。

他說：「婆婆會很想見到妳的。」

這個拜訪的想法，可是讓海蒂興奮極了。

p. 34 接下來的幾天，拜訪彼得家的念頭在海蒂腦海裡揮之不去，她不斷地拜託爺爺帶她去見見婆婆。

有天海蒂說：「我今天一定要過去，不然婆婆會等得不耐煩。」

阿爾卑斯伯伯便到閣樓拿了條厚毛毯，說：「那就走吧。」

他倆一起走到了門外，阿爾卑斯伯伯拖出雪橇，坐了上去，然後用毛毯把海蒂裹了起來，一手抱在懷裡，接著雙腳一推，雪橇便開始滑下山坡。

雪橇滑得極快，海蒂彷彿覺得自己就是隻在天空飛翔的小鳥，高興地放聲大叫。

他們不久便到達婆婆的小屋，阿爾卑斯伯伯要她進去屋內，天黑前要回家，説完就離開，回山上去了。

p. 36–37　海蒂進到小屋後，看見一位正在織布的年邁婦人，心想那一定就是彼得的奶奶了。她走向老婦人，開始自我介紹，她説：「婆婆，您好嗎？我是海蒂。」

　　婆婆找了找海蒂的手，握在自己手裡説：「妳就是跟阿爾卑斯伯伯住在一起的小姑娘嗎？」

　　「是的，我就是。」她環視屋內，發現窗葉鬆開，便要婆婆去瞧瞧。

　　年邁婦人説：「我看不見。」

　　海蒂震驚極了，替婆婆感到非常難過而開始大哭：「有沒有人可以幫妳重見光明？」還在哽咽的她一邊説著。

　　「孩子啊，別哭。跟我説，妳覺得到現在這裡的生活還好嗎？」婆婆説。

　　海蒂擦乾眼淚，將她和爺爺一起生活的點點滴滴全都告訴婆婆，那天她們倆聊得非常愉快。

　　隔天，海蒂與爺爺一起來到婆婆的屋中，要幫忙修理窗葉。

　　海蒂向婆婆説明情況：「我爺爺會替妳修好窗葉喔。」

　　阿爾卑斯伯伯先檢查過窗葉，就開始修理了。

　　海蒂幾乎每天都來探視婆婆，她們倆變得很要好。

　　只要聽見海蒂的腳步聲，奶奶便會高興地呼喊：「感謝老天！那孩子來了。」

[第五章] 離開阿爾卑斯山

p. 38 兩年過去了，有天，蒂提阿姨突然出現，要帶海蒂離開，這真是讓她感到錯愕。阿爾卑斯伯伯不想讓她走，兩個大人因此起了爭執。

「海蒂都八歲了，還不識字，我要帶她到法蘭克福的有錢人家裡去。」

「妳給我閉嘴！」爺爺吼著說。

「那戶人家有個瘸子女兒，海蒂可以當她的玩伴，順便學習識字。」

阿爾卑斯伯伯聽都不想聽她的解釋，就說：「妳說完沒有？」

「這種機會可是千載難逢呢。」蒂提又說。

p. 40–41 「隨妳便！帶她走，害了她吧。」阿爾卑斯伯伯告誡完，氣沖沖地走了。

海蒂說：「妳惹爺爺生氣囉。」

蒂提阿姨嘆了口氣說：「他會沒事的。」

海蒂根本不想走，可是蒂提阿姨向她保證很快就會帶她回來，所以便動身離開下山。路上，她們遇見了彼得。

彼得問：「妳要去哪裏？」

「我要去法蘭克福了，我一定要跟婆婆說聲再見。」海蒂說。

蒂提急著下山，拉著她說：「沒時間了。」

彼得匆匆趕回家中，說：「她要把海蒂帶走了。」

婆婆焦急地問：「是誰要帶走我的孩子？」

等不及彼得回答，婆婆就打開窗戶高聲一呼：「海蒂！」

「那是婆婆。我一定要當面跟她道別。」海蒂說。

蒂提說：「我們還要趕去火車站，妳之後再帶個禮物給她吧。」

「我要送什麼給她？」

「黑麵包對她來說太難咬了，或許可以送些軟的白麵包捲吧。」

海蒂就這樣離開了。阿爾卑斯伯伯變得比以往更暴躁，村民對他又益加畏懼了。

不過婆婆總會告訴人們他對海蒂有多好，還有他幫忙修繕窗葉的事情。兩人都非常地思念海蒂。

[第六章] 在法蘭克福

p. 42–43 法蘭克福的有錢人家住在大宅第中，屋主是謝斯曼先生，他的妻子於幾年前去世，而女兒克萊拉則因病需坐輪椅。

謝斯曼先生常因工作不在家，便把管理屋子的權力交給洛頓梅爾小姐，而她則成了總管，掌管宅內的大小事。

她對每件事情嚴格規定的作風，讓同事都對她很畏懼，她就有點像是當家的。

打從蒂堤跟海蒂到達之後，洛頓梅爾小姐就不怎麼高興。首先是因為克萊拉大了海蒂四歲，但她早就特別說過要的是一位和克萊拉同樣是十二歲的女孩。

她也訝異海蒂並不識字。對她而言，海蒂的水準跟克萊拉比起來，可是天差地遠。

p. 44–45 洛頓梅爾小姐嗤之以鼻地說：「妳是從窮鄉僻壤找來這女孩的嗎？」她想換掉海蒂，找個更合適的人選，但蒂堤隨口編個理由，一溜煙地離開屋中。

洛頓梅爾小姐一度還搞不清楚狀況，隨後才追了出去，不過已經來不及，蒂堤早不見人影了。

海蒂還站在門旁，克萊拉目睹整個會面的過程，她對海蒂說：「過來啊，海蒂。妳喜歡法蘭克福嗎？」

「我不喜歡。我明天就要回家，還要帶些軟綿綿的白麵包捲送給婆婆。」

「妳這女生還真是有趣，妳是來這陪我的，我們要一起唸書，亞瑟先生會教妳識字，很好玩的呦。」

當天晚上，洛頓梅爾小姐教了海蒂在家裡應守的規矩還有適宜的行為，可是海蒂根本無法聽進她囉嗦的長串規定。

她一心只想著餐桌上的白麵包捲，還偷偷放了幾個在她的口袋裡。

她心想：「婆婆一定會很開心！」

p. 47 隔天海蒂醒來，一開始，她完全想不起來自己身在何處，身邊的事物都顯得很陌生，過了一會兒才想起昨天發生的事。

海蒂想要打開窗戶，感受陽光的溫暖，但窗子太高，沒辦法開，此時她感到失望又拘束，她想念山上的那個家。

每天早上海蒂跟克萊拉都會跟亞瑟先生上課，他教海蒂英文字母。在上了好幾堂的字母課程後，海蒂還是記不起來所有字母，那對她來説真的太複雜了。

　　通常在下午時，克萊拉會小憩一下，海蒂愛幹什麼都行，只要不闖禍就好。

p. 48–49 到了晚上，海蒂會説她在山上的事情給克萊拉聽，説越多有關阿爾卑斯山的事，她就越鍾愛那遙遠山上的所有人事物。

　　海蒂時常表示：「我明天一定要回家。」不過克萊拉總是説些安慰人的話來安撫她，還有要送給婆婆而越積越多的白麵包捲，也讓她留了下來。

　　偶爾海蒂也會忍不住想回家的念頭。有次她打包好行李，決心要離開，就在門口遇到了洛頓梅爾小姐。

　　洛頓梅爾小姐知道海蒂的意圖後，氣急敗壞地責備她：「就這樣跑掉很沒禮貌！妳這個忘恩負義的小孩。」

　　因此海蒂又留了下來。那天晚餐，洛頓梅爾小姐不時注意著海蒂，不過沒什麼淘氣的行為發生，她除了拿走白麵包捲以外，餐點幾乎都沒動過。

［第七章］謝斯曼先生與奶奶

p. 50–51 一日，謝斯曼先生出差回到家中，沒等到僕人替他卸下行李，便逕自往克萊拉的房間走去。

克萊拉深愛父親，很興奮見到他，父女倆問候親吻彼此，這時海蒂害羞地站在一旁的角落。

「妳一定就是我們的那位瑞士小姑娘吧。快過來，妳們倆變成好朋友了嗎？」謝斯曼先生詢問。

海蒂回答：「是的，克萊拉待我很好。」

到了晚上，洛頓梅爾小姐向謝斯曼先生一一訴說海蒂的種種粗俗行徑，但他似乎不打算追究，洛頓梅爾小姐心生不悅，卻也只能順從謝斯曼先生的指示。

p. 52 兩週後，謝斯曼先生離開家中，克萊拉的奶奶前來探望。海蒂早在奶奶來拜訪前，就聽說這位年邁女士的種種事情，克萊拉平時都稱呼她「奶奶」，所以海蒂也就跟著這樣叫。

奶奶是一位善良慈愛的婦人，她對孩子友善的態度迅速建立起她與海蒂之間的親密友誼。

有天下午，奶奶拿了本裡頭有各地風景圖的故事書給海蒂看，海蒂發現書中有提到她山上的生活，還有一張牧羊人和羊隻在草原上的圖片，她看著看著就哭了起來。

p. 54–55 奶奶深知海蒂的問題，為了鼓勵她，奶奶承諾要把書送她當作獎勵，但海蒂可要先學會識字才行。

雖然不怎麼明白奶奶的意思，海蒂還是點了點頭，這時她想到彼得識字的困難，現在她總算懂得那是什麼感覺。

奶奶要海蒂相信自己，因為與海蒂同年的孩子學習識字，多數沒什麼大問題。

海蒂又點了點頭，繼續啜泣，她不能告訴奶奶她想回家，洛頓梅爾小姐說過的話——「逃跑的忘恩負義孩子」她還言猶在耳。

奶奶說：「孩子啊，妳有時看起來悶悶不樂的，或許妳不想讓別人知道妳在難過什麼，但妳隨時能向上帝祈禱，不需要是個虔誠信徒，神就會賜給妳幸福與喜樂。」

一個禮拜過後，亞瑟先生告知奶奶海蒂識字的成果。

亞瑟先生充滿信心地高聲說著：「我在她身上花費時間與精神證明是值得的！她現在讀起字來跟以前比真是好多了！」

而這當然不只是亞瑟先生的教導，還有奶奶提供獎勵的策略奏效，讓海蒂持續學習，她也是功勞一份呢。

p. 56 儘管如此，奶奶聽到亞瑟先生說的話還是很興奮，當晚，她便按照約定將書送給了海蒂。

「這本書現在是妳的了。」奶奶說。

那本書成了海蒂最珍貴的資產，她喜愛極了書中的圖片，還實際運用她的閱讀技巧，朗讀書中的故事給克萊拉和奶奶聽。

奶奶的來訪很快就結束了，冬去春來，海蒂滿臉愁容。

「彼得現在一定帶著山羊在草地上。」她心想。

她越想到老家的事物，鄉愁就越濃。

p. 57 有一天早上，謝斯曼大宅發生了件怪事，僕人們發現大門是打開的，但沒有人承認是誰開的門。奇怪的是，屋中也沒有東西失竊。

接連下來的幾個早上，僕人一再發現門被打開。

一天夜裡，兩個僕人決定要留下來瞧瞧。接近午夜十二點時，僕人房外傳來奇怪的聲響，他們匆忙跑去查看，看見樓梯那兒有個白色人影。

他們想再看仔細些，人卻一下就不見了，這簡直嚇死他們了。

p. 58–59 僕人們向洛頓梅爾小姐報告前晚所發現的事情，雖然沒有證據，白色人影卻讓他們聯想到鬼魂。

驚嚇不已的洛頓梅爾小姐捎了一封信，請求謝斯曼先生需立即返家，以確保家中安全。

謝斯曼先生不相信鬼魂的存在，他對僕人們的聯想感到啼笑皆非，但還是在幾天後返回家中。

他取笑洛頓梅爾小姐的膽小和小題大做，不過還是保證會不睡覺，親自去見見「鬼魂」。

那晚極度安靜，在接近午夜十二點時，他聽到些聲響便走了出去，看到了一個白色身影。

「是誰？」他大喊。

那身影轉過身，大聲尖叫，謝斯曼先生看見那臉非常訝異，那正是穿著白色睡袍的海蒂。

「妳怎麼會在這裡，孩子？」

「我……我不知道。」海蒂結結巴巴地說。

「過來這裡，我們談談。」謝斯曼先生安慰地說。

經由一番談話，他知道了海蒂的主要問題所在，她並非惡意計劃逃跑，而只是想家。

p. 60–61 她每晚都夢到家鄉的人事物，而太過想家的影響才讓她夢遊。

隔天，謝斯曼先生同意讓海蒂回家，克萊拉極力反對此事。

她試著要阻止父親做下決定，但父親在溝通過程中說服了她。

「我們不能只顧自己，也許這對海蒂才是最好的。」謝斯曼先生又說：「明年再讓妳去拜訪海蒂就是了。」

克萊拉在海蒂的行李籃中打包了許多東西，又放了一大堆白麵包捲。

這時，蒂堤阿姨也到達了，她受委託要帶海蒂回到瑞士去。海蒂真是開心極了，她向克萊拉與謝斯曼先生道謝告別後，就離開了。

能回到瑞士的阿爾卑斯山上，海蒂雀躍無比。她順道拜訪彼得的家，見到了在屋裡的婆婆。

p. 63 婆婆聽見開門的聲音，說：「唉，海蒂以前老這樣進屋的。」

「婆婆，我回來囉！」

「噢，感謝主！是妳，妳回來了！」婆婆流著淚地說。

「婆婆，妳不要哭。我替妳帶了些白麵包捲，以後不用再吃硬梆梆的黑麵包了。」海蒂將白麵包捲放在婆婆腿上。

婆婆欣喜若狂地大聲説著:「孩子啊,有妳真是我的福氣。」

海蒂握住婆婆的手,並説:「我要去找爺爺了,不過我明天會再來喔。」

p. 64 海蒂攀爬上一樣熟悉的小路,看見爺爺就在小屋外頭,跑了過去,緊緊抱住了他。

她高興地大聲呼喊:「爺爺!爺爺!爺爺!」

「妳還是回來啦?」爺爺説。

爺爺給了她一碗羊奶,海蒂心滿意足地一飲而盡,大呼:「爺爺,還是我們家的羊奶最好喝了!」

她在法蘭克福時,不時夢想著這天到來,而現在,她的美夢成真了,海蒂跟爺爺都很開心。

當晚,爺爺還跑到閣樓,看海蒂入的睡模樣有十次之多呢。

[第九章] 克萊拉來訪

p. 66-67 海蒂離開後,便常與克萊拉以信件問候彼此,克萊拉在信中承諾,在隔年春天要前來拜訪。

海蒂非常期待再見到克萊拉,她想要帶克萊拉在家鄉四處走走,不過冬天好漫長,海蒂偶爾等得也有點累,幸好有些事情讓她閒不下來。

首先,她要上學,還要探望婆婆,説故事給她聽,海蒂的閱讀能力讓婆婆很驚訝。

此外,彼得也在海蒂的教導之下,在班上成績有所進步,到了冬末,彼得已經可以閱讀一些程度簡單的聖歌文章了。

春天總算來了,阿爾卑斯山上滿山蒼翠。有天,彼得拿來了一封信給海蒂。

海蒂讀著信高興地大聲説著:「是克萊拉寄的,她不久後就要來了!」

彼得聽見後，心頭一陣忌妒，他轉過身，猛力砰地一聲關了身後的門。

　　p. 68–69 克萊拉來訪當天，海蒂看見山間路上有來訪者的隊伍，克萊拉就坐在由兩名壯漢抬著的轎上，而奶奶騎在馬上，還有位小伙子扛著克萊拉的輪椅，跟搬運著被子毛皮、大包小包的搬運工。

　　「他們來囉！」海蒂大聲喊著，開心地上上下下一直跳。

　　來訪者不久後到達小屋，兩位小姑娘高興地招呼彼此，奶奶下了馬後，向阿爾卑斯伯伯打聲招呼。

　　她接著對海蒂説：「海蒂，妳氣色可真好！」

　　爺爺將克萊拉從轎上一把抱到輪椅上，海蒂推著她去看看羊舍、冷杉，還有翠綠茂盛的青草地。

　　「海蒂，這可真美！」克萊拉驚呼。

　　「這些才不算什麼，」海蒂説：「上頭餵養羊的地方還更美呢。」

　　午餐時，克萊拉驚呼：「這裡的東西好吃多了。」

　　阿爾卑斯伯伯抓住機會，對奶奶説：「我們想留克萊拉下來一起渡過夏天，山上的空氣對她也有好處。」

　　「噢，我可愛的伯伯，」奶奶説：「我剛剛也有這念頭呢，真不知道該怎麼謝你。」

　　「好耶！」兩個小女生大喊。

　　接近黃昏時，奶奶便跟搬運工人一同離開了。阿爾卑斯伯伯在海蒂床邊也為克萊拉鋪了個床，一樣可以從圓窗中，一覽無遺山中景色與滿天夜空。

p. 71 每天都有一連串的郊遊等著海蒂跟克萊拉，海蒂會推著輪椅，帶克萊拉去摘摘花，或是一起閒話家常、寫信給奶奶。

克萊拉也結識了彼得，但彼得卻視她為眼中釘，他覺得自己好像在跟克萊拉爭寵。

平時彼得是個個性溫和的男孩子，但這次，他的怒火與妒火中燒讓他益加無法忍受。

有次他怒火爆發，以雙手把克萊拉的輪椅亂搖一通後便跑走。

但這並沒有消除或是減少他的怒氣，他依然氣憤難平，並且非常想念他的同伴。

[第十章] 克萊拉能走路了！

p. 72–73 有天早上，克萊拉說：「若能走路，我多希望可以到山上看看青草地啊。」

「克萊拉，妳現在看起來健壯多了，要不要試試站在地上，一次就好？」阿爾卑斯伯伯問。

「我不能百分之百確定行不行，這樣會痛。」克萊拉說。

「試試看，我會扶著妳。」阿爾卑斯伯伯保證著。

克萊拉扶著阿爾卑斯伯伯的手臂，將自己從輪椅上拉了起來。她在過程中搖搖晃晃，不時失去平衡，但不靠枴杖或任何器具，她還是辦到了，現在就直挺挺地站在地上。

「太棒了，克萊拉！」海蒂開心地大聲嚷嚷。

隔天早上，彼得路過阿爾卑斯伯伯的小屋，他沒吹哨子，輕聲往阿爾卑斯伯伯的羊舍走去，馬上映入他眼簾的是克萊拉的輪椅。

彼得怒不可抑地走向輪椅，用力一推，輪椅就這麼搖搖晃晃地滾落山下，一眨眼便消失在山邊。

由於罪惡感使然，彼得沒帶到阿爾卑斯伯伯的羊隻就匆忙跑上山去了。

p. 74–75 幾分鐘後，海蒂從小屋中出來。

海蒂問：「輪椅呢？」

「羊怎麼還在羊舍裡，彼得呢？」阿爾卑斯伯伯生氣地說。

克萊拉傷心地說：「少了輪椅，我再沒辦法看見草原了。」

「別擔心，我揹妳上去。」阿爾卑斯伯伯說。

三人到達草原後，見到彼得帶著羊隻在那兒。

阿爾卑斯伯伯問彼得輪椅的下落，彼得卻辯稱：「什麼輪椅啊？我不知道。」

伯伯沒再多說什麼，只拿了午餐袋給兩位小姑娘後就離開了。

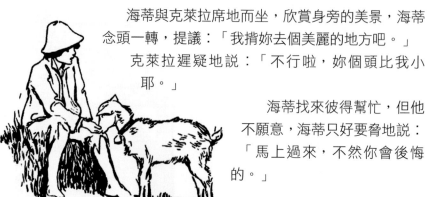

海蒂與克萊拉席地而坐，欣賞身旁的美景，海蒂念頭一轉，提議：「我揹妳去個美麗的地方吧。」

克萊拉遲疑地說：「不行啦，妳個頭比我小耶。」

海蒂找來彼得幫忙，但他不願意，海蒂只好要脅地說：「馬上過來，不然你會後悔的。」

聽見海蒂這麼說，破壞克萊拉輪椅的罪惡感使他聽從海蒂的指示。

起初，克萊拉感到害怕，接著她便起身想要向前走幾步，疼痛難耐的她哭了起來，卻依然吃力地又走了幾步。

學走路對克萊拉而言就跟打仗一樣，不過她決心要做出承諾，為了感謝朋友的善意與鼓勵，她一定要獨立行走。

「很好！再來一次！專心地跟著我就好。」海蒂鼓勵著。

p. 76 她跨出一步又一步，最後，海蒂跟彼得放開了克萊拉。

「海蒂，妳看！現在我能走路了！」克萊拉喜極而泣地喊著。

跟著克萊拉緩慢而平穩的步伐，他們到達花草繁盛的景點，一起度過下半天。

幾天過後，克萊拉搖晃不定的步伐越來越穩了，每一天她都感到越來越不費力，也能走得更遠些。

奶奶幾天之後就要來接她回家，她決定要用這天大的好消息來給奶奶一個驚喜。

[第十一章] 奇蹟發生

p. 78 奶奶來訪的那個早晨，克萊拉與海蒂就坐在長椅子上等她的到來。等奶奶一到達時，克萊拉便牽著海蒂的手站了起來。

兩個小女孩一同走向奶奶。一開始，奶奶相當詫異，眼前的克萊拉就像變了一個人似的。

奶奶喜極而泣，跑向她們，先擁抱了克萊拉，又擁著海蒂，又再度抱緊了克萊拉，高興地無法言語。

最後終於大喊了聲：「感謝主！這真是個奇蹟！」

p. 80–81 奶奶對阿爾卑斯伯伯說：「親愛的伯伯呀！我們要怎麼謝你呢！這奇蹟不靠醫療或任何設備，憑的是你的苦心和照顧啊！」

「是陽光還有山上的空氣幫的忙。」阿爾卑斯伯伯微笑說著。

「沒錯，還有我們家的山羊奶呢。」海蒂接著說。

此時，滿臉侷促不安與歉疚的彼得走了過來，對奶奶說：「對不起！這全摔碎了。」

奶奶一臉疑惑地問：「這孩子是怎麼回事？」

「我想，他就是弄丟克萊拉輪椅的始作俑者。」阿爾卑斯伯伯說。

奶奶這才恍然大悟，了解彼得話中的意思，並說：「做壞事的人都該得到懲罰，不過彼得的行為讓克萊拉能夠行走，這次反而成了件好事。

彼得，答應我，你會反省過錯，不再做壞事，凡事三思而後行。」

彼得點點頭，保證會改過自新。

「拿去，我要你記住法蘭克福的人。」說著便拿了一元給彼得。

彼得無法相信自己不但沒被懲罰，反而還得到報酬。

p. 82–83 「海蒂，妳呢？妳想要什麼禮物？」奶奶溫柔地詢問。

海蒂稍微想了想，說：「我要給婆婆一個床，跟我在法蘭克福睡的一樣的那種，這樣她就不用再睡在又硬又冷的床上了。」

「我一回到法蘭克福，就立刻送來最高級的床墊。」奶奶允諾。馬車正在山腳下等著奶奶與克萊拉，由於克萊拉無法冒險行走遠遠的山路，阿爾卑斯伯伯便揹著她下山。

克萊拉很捨不得離開，承諾明年夏天會再度前來。

「夏天很快就來了，我們再一起到草原上，一定很好玩的！」海蒂說。

海蒂與爺爺目送馬車離開，她追著馬車大喊：「明年夏天再見了，克萊拉！」

Answers

P. 90   **A**   **1** c   **2** b   **3** a   **4** c
           5 b   **6** a   **7** a   **8** c   **9** c

P. 92   **B**   __2__ ⇨ __1__ ⇨ __3__ ⇨ __4__

P. 93   **C**   **1** turn   **11** at

               2 cry   **12** in

               3 responsibility   **13** up

               4 slice   **14** on

               5 ensured   **15** opposing

               6 deal   **16** passed away

               7 released   **17** awfully

               8 to   **18** popularity

               9 about   **19** situation

               10 over

P. 95   **D** The servants reported to Miss Rottenmeier about their findings the previous night.

海蒂：阿爾卑斯山的小女孩【二版】
Heidi

作者 _ 約翰娜·施皮里
　　　（Johanna Spyri）
改寫 _ Andrew Chien
審訂 _ Dennis Le Boeuf/Liming Jing
插圖 _ 小白魚
翻譯／編輯 _ 謝雅婷／黃朝萍
校對 _ 賴祖兒
編輯協力／洪巧玲／周演音
封面設計 _ 林書玉
排版 _ 葳豐／林書玉
製程管理 _ 洪巧玲
發行人 _ 周均亮
出版者 _ 寂天文化事業股份有限公司
電話 _ +886-2-2365-9739
傳真 _ +886-2-2365-9835
網址 _ www.icosmos.com.tw
讀者服務 _ onlineservice@icosmos.com.tw
出版日期 _ 2020年7月 二版一刷 　　（250201）
郵撥帳號 _ 1998620-0 寂天文化事業股份有限公司

國家圖書館出版品預行編目資料

海蒂：阿爾卑斯山的小女孩 / Johanna Spyri原著；
Andrew Chien改寫. -- 二版. -- [臺北市] : 寂天文化,
2020.07
　　面；　公分. -- (Grade 4經典文學讀本)
譯自：Heidi
ISBN 978-986-318-924-4(25K平裝附光碟片)

1.英語　2.讀本
805.18　　　　　　　　　　109009009